MW00935731

Mountain Time

donna coulson

Copyright © 2012 by donna coulson
First edition August 2013
Second edition October 2016

ISBN-10: 1537774212
ISBN-13: 9781537774213

cover photographs by donna coulson.
The front cover photo is the view from near Bridger Peak down the valley that includes Rudefeha Mine, Dillon townsite and Haggarty Gulch.The back cover is a different view of the same valley.It's what Nathan called the "valley of ghosts".

All rights reserved.

No part of this publication may be reproduced in any form, or by any means, electronic or mechanical, including photocopying, recording, or any information browsing, storage, or retrieval system, without permission in writing from the author.

For Karl,
I am so thankful for you.
I love you like breathing.

God is beyond time.

He is in it, yet above and outside it.

"For my thoughts are not your thoughts, neither are your ways my ways," declares the Lord. As the heavens are higher than the earth, so are my ways higher than your ways and my thoughts than your thoughts. As the rain and the snow come down from heaven, and do not return to it without watering the earth and making it bud and flourish, so that it yields seed for the sower and bread for the eater, so is my word that goes out from my mouth: It will not return to me empty, but will accomplish what I desire and achieve the purpose for which I sent it. You will go out in joy and be led forth in peace; the mountains and hills will burst into song before you and all the trees of the field will clap their hands.

Isaiah 55:8-12 NIV

Chapter 1

June 17, 1902

Andriette could hardly hear the train whistle over the pounding of her heart. Three days on the train made her weary and tired, she felt grimy and disheveled. Eleven months of planning and praying and hoping and fearing were focused on this day. *Father God,* she started to pray and then stopped. She didn't know what to say. She had been very certain that God was leading her in this journey, but now that she was arriving, she was terrified and at the same time ashamed of her fear and lack of faith.

She tried again. *Father,* she stopped. Words just wouldn't come. Her mind was racing and uncertainty was rising. She took a deep breath and closed her eyes. *Father God, I'm scared. Thy will be done. Amen.* She took another breath and opened her eyes. Her heart was still pounding and her hands were sweaty, but she felt a bit more under control. The panic faded to manageable.

Andriette looked out the train window. They were almost at the station. She had traveled across Nebraska and southern Wyoming for a day and a half, so the lack of trees and green didn't shock her. The station was small, just a platform and a small station house. There were perhaps twenty or twenty five people standing around waiting for the train. Some of them were dressed in railroad uniforms and some were obviously passengers, surrounded by boxes and trunks waiting to get on the train. She was still too far away to see any faces. What she could see of the town wasn't impressive. It wouldn't have mattered if it turned out to be an opulent paradise. She knew that she wouldn't be staying in Rawlins long.

As the train slowed, her eyes scanned the people on the platform. There was no need to get out the worn tintype picture she carried with her. She had memorized every detail of that face. Yet now that she was here, she was frightened that they would not recognize one another, or that he met some kind of delay and wasn't there. Or worse, that he had changed his mind and wasn't coming. Her heart began to pound again, and once more she took a deep breath and prayed. This time she didn't even try for words, just a quick connection to God to recapture some semblance of peace in her heart and mind. It worked.

The train came to a slow gentle stop and the conductor boomed, "Rawlins, Wyoming." Andriette stood, a little shaky, frowning that her dress was wrinkled and dusty from the trip. She smoothed her hair and checked to make sure her hat was on straight, took a deep breath and picked up her pocketbook and satchel, and then walked down the aisle of the train. She stopped for a moment at the door, trying to square her shoulders and look confident, quite sure she wasn't succeeding. Feeling lost and unsure, she looked around though actually seeing nothing thanks to her nerves, then the conductor reached to help her down the steps and she took his hand.

For all the times she'd imagined this moment, her confidence drained from her and she felt exposed and alone. Panic threatened to overtake her. She took a few steps forward. Her eyes scanned the people on the platform. She felt ill for a moment, shaky with weak and watery legs. She scanned the crowd again. No one met her eyes, no one noticed her at all.

He stood waiting by the corner of the building at the back of the platform, rooted to the same spot for nearly two hours. He too, barely heard the train whistle announcing the train's arrival thanks to the pounding of his heart. He watched as the train came to a stop and the conductor stepped out and set the wooden step by the train's door. With every passenger that came down the stairs his heart leaped and then fell as he realized that it wasn't her. When she did come through the door, hesitating for a moment on the threshold before starting down the steps, his heart stopped. He knew her in an instant and was overpowered by his first glimpse. The photo of her in his breast pocket was two years old. It didn't show the golden highlights in her brown hair or the bright green of her eyes. In his mind's eye he pictured her taller than her five foot three inch frame. He struggled to breathe and couldn't remember to make his feet move. She was beautiful.

She looked around, trying to focus. People were moving all around her, some greeting passengers who were stepping off the train and others preparing to get on. She stopped in the middle of the platform and took a breath. *Breathing and praying is all I can seem to do,* she thought, and that thought made her smile to herself.

It was the smile that did it. He stared and was studying her. When she smiled, it finally dawned on him that he needed to move. He stepped forward, surprised that he could. His confidence returned and he went to meet her.

She saw him then. He was tall, slender, and wore brown pants and boots and a denim shirt. His hat was in his hand and his boots were scuffed, but he was clean and neat. His sandy brown hair was a little long, and it was clear that he didn't often take off his hat, because his forehead was very white compared to the deep tan of the rest of his face. When he was still about two strides away from her, he smiled. In that moment, her world brightened and her heart did a small somersault.

Months later, when they talked about their first meeting, neither could remember what their first words were. They remembered collecting the two trunks she brought with her.

She especially remembered how he lifted each one so easily and carried it to his waiting buckboard. He remembered how quiet she was but that her eyes followed him and seemed to gather in everything.

He reached for her satchel, to add it to the trunks in the buckboard, but she shook her head. "Is it alright with you if I keep this with me?"

"Sure," was his answer, "May I carry it for you?"

She hesitated, and then answered, "I would appreciate it, thank you."

"Are you hungry, Ma'am?"

She smiled, "Yes, actually I am." He liked the way she met his eyes.

"I'll walk you over to Ducolon's café. It has what I think is the best food in Rawlins. If you don't mind, you could have something to drink while I go to stable the horses and wagon."

"Stable them?"

"I arrived in Rawlins this morning, and the horses are tired. Trains around here aren't famous for running on time, and I didn't want to be late. The trip back up to the mountains isn't an easy one and you've already endured a long journey. I thought you might need a day to rest, and I need to get supplies bought and loaded, so I got us a place to stay at the hotel."

Her heart flipped towards panic again. He read it in her eyes and added, "I got us two rooms, Miss Andriette. I don't want to rush you or take anything for granted."

Breathe, she thought to herself, *breathe*! She knew her voice would be shaky if she spoke, so she simply smiled at him and took his arm.

Sitting in the café alone while she waited for him to return gave her some time to gather herself and reflect. She watched the activity in the street outside the window at first. Rawlins was larger than she'd expected, though it was still a small place. A sign across the street announced a picnic to celebrate the founding of Rawlins twenty years earlier when the transcontinental railroad pushed through on its way west. She watched people bustling by the window as her thoughts turned to Nathan. Nathan Jameson. She'd said his name a thousand times, and now she was here. He wasn't exactly handsome, but he was attractive in his own way – *or am I just telling myself that?* He looked like his picture, so his features were not a surprise. His voice was deeper than she'd imagined. She liked how when he smiled, his eyes smiled as well. He was taller and broader than she expected, and she felt small as she walked beside him.

So far, his manners and behavior were gentlemanly and polite, and she felt like she might be able to relax around him soon. She kept her satchel and pocketbook with her, and looked down at them beside her. Beside a few personal items and the dress she planned to wear later, the satchel contained her most treasured possessions: her Bible, the necklace her aunts gave her on her sixteenth birthday, the money she saved up for the last two years by working as a house maid for the Millers, and the letters. She was thinking about the letters when he returned to the table and sat down opposite her.

"After we eat, I need to go to the mercantile and buy supplies. If you aren't too tired, I'd like it if you would go with me. I am sure there will be things you'd like to add to my list, and I need your help." He stopped as the waitress brought them plates filled with slices of beef roast and mashed potatoes.

He hesitated, looked at the plate and then at her. "I'll say a quick blessing if you don't mind?" She nodded and bowed her head. "Thank you, Lord for this food and for Andriette arriving safely. Amen."

His simple words touched her and for a moment she thought she might cry. *Don't be a silly girl!* She yelled silently at herself, *He needs a grown up woman, not a crying schoolgirl!* She fiddled with the pocketbook she held in her lap, the moment passed and she gained control.

When she looked up, he was studying her. "Did I do something wrong Ma'am? I do like to pray before I eat, but I don't like to call a lot of attention to myself in a public place. I'm sorry if I offended you or made you unhappy."

His eyes were serious and concerned. "Oh no, you didn't do anything wrong. I feel exactly the same way about praying in public. No, your prayer was perfect and I was touched by it."

He relaxed a little then. "I guess we both are a little nervous here," he added. "I haven't eaten since yesterday, and I know I'm hungry, but my stomach feels like I swallowed a bird, it keeps fluttering around. I am really happy you are here, and I want you to be happy. I've looked forward to you getting here for so long, and I want everything to be perfect. Since you've arrived, I look at this town and me, through what I imagine your eyes are seeing, and it isn't much. A rowdy end-of-track town and a dusty hick."

Her eyes never left his face. This was the honest, real man she'd met and gotten to know through his letters. *How can I tell him that?* she wondered. "Nathan," she began. "What I've seen of Rawlins so far is rough and rowdy, and we both are dusty, but only on the surface. If you have been honest with me in your letters, and I feel that you have, then neither of us has anything to be worried about."

He grinned then, a real grin, and he picked up his fork.

Andriette was surprised a few minutes later to look down at her plate and find that the food was gone. She had been hungry, too. The waitress refilled Nathan's coffee cup and asked if they wanted pie. Nathan looked up from his plate and met her eyes, then answered yes for both of them. He seemed nervous again.

The waitress brought them each a slice of cherry pie. It looked wonderful. Nathan hesitated, with his fork in his hand. He laid his fork back down and spoke softly, so only Andriette could hear. "I don't want to push you or rush you into anything you don't want to do. It is early June, though, and I have work to do at home. The trip from here to my place will take us four days of hard travelling, and I hoped to leave tomorrow. I am the kind of man who needs to have a plan. This is what I have in my mind, and I need to lay it out for you so you can tell me what you think and want." He took a deep breath and looked at her.

This was an important moment and they both knew it. "Nathan, we are strangers in some ways and the closest of friends in others. I have told you things about myself and my thoughts that no other person knows. But I have only known your face an hour. I am scared, and I am nervous, but I haven't seen or heard anything so far that makes me think you are anyone but who you showed me you were in your letters. I think we need to complete our preparations here and start for home tomorrow, just as you'd planned."

He looked shocked and jubilant at the same time. "I like how you said that, Ma'am. I agree, let's start for home tomorrow!"

Once more he picked up his fork and then put it down. The seriousness was back. "Andriette, I am a man of faith, and I know we both share that. I am not willing to take you into the mountains to our new home if everything isn't right." He reached forward and took her hand, the first time he actually touched her. "Andriette, before we leave tomorrow morning, will you accompany me to the courthouse and become my wife?"

Of course, it was what they had planned. The people back home who knew her intentions teased her about being a 'mail-order bride'. Her father was horrified and scoffed at the idea, making her feel cheap and unworthy in the process. Andriette stood up to his controlling and mean spirited jibes, though, because she knew that there was nothing hasty, improper or ill-advised about her decision to leave a place where she'd never felt loved or needed in order to be with a man who knew her heart and wanted her.

"Yes, Nathan, I will be proud to become your wife in the morning."

Chapter 2

August 17, 2007

She had never sat alone at the top of the world before. Scores of times she enjoyed the view from this very spot, but never alone. The trip was a challenge. The road was perfect for a Jeep or a four-wheeler, but her little Chevy Cavalier found the whole experience humbling. She finally showed it mercy, left it beside the track, and hiked the rest of the way.

She'd always thought of Bridger Peak, elevation 11,003 feet, to be the top of the world, a place of wonder and blessing, a seemingly magical place she shared with her dad. Now, she sat here alone, absorbing the beauty in the 360 degree vista. The air was crisp and clean. She imagined that if she wanted, she could just take a bite of it and the sweet juices of morning would run down her chin. The picture made her smile, and she began to feel the wounds deep in her soul begin, ever so slightly to heal.

If anyone had been watching her, and no one was yet, they would have thought this woman to be out of place in this rugged country. Hannah startled people with her loveliness. Streaks of gold illuminated her light brown hair as the sun of the late morning caught it. Her blue eyes were oval and rimmed with long lashes. Usually her smile was quick and could lift the spirits of anyone around. She wasn't beautiful by *Vogue* standards, but her confidence and quick humor were as much a part of her attractiveness as her straight thin nose and tall, lithe figure.

Watchers would have also wondered at how still she sat, there at the top of the peak. For close to two hours she barely moved. Her thoughts were alive though, and sometimes they jumped so fast from one memory to the next that she became breathless.

Hannah grew up in a normal, happy home on a quiet neighborhood street in Omaha, Nebraska. She was good in school, took dance classes and argued about the piano lessons her mother insisted upon. She had friends and, beginning in high school, boyfriends that her father met at the door with a stern look and a presence that scared them into treating her well whether they originally intended to or not. Her memories of her childhood and teen years were punctuated with another life, though, a life that included mostly just her father and herself and a small cabin tucked back into the woods and high mountains of southern Wyoming. Once a year for a week and sometimes two, she and Dad loaded the pickup truck with food and blankets and cinnamon bears and took off.

***

Her first trip was when she was eight. Before that, her mother thought she was too little and her father acquiesced. They left on July 5th, but the adventure started long before that on snowy nights when Dad tucked her into bed and told her stories. He'd always done that, but that winter his stories were different. He told her about a place called Dillon. A place that now was a ghost town but was once an amazing little town at the top of the Continental Divide. He talked of tough men who drove teams of horses and mules, sometimes fifteen at once, up rough trails to take supplies to other men who were working in mines digging copper. Dad's stories were so vivid and alive that Hannah could see the men and hear the creak of the leather. She could picture the women, in their long skirts, making a life for themselves and their families.

When that summer finally came and they hugged Mom good-bye and started for the mountains, Hannah felt like she was as close friends to the people who had lived in Dillon as those who lived on her street.

Hannah sat, thinking about the first trip. She could feel the crisp mountain air as she stepped out of the pickup and looked at their cabin for the first time. It wasn't anything fancy. Her father purchased an old mining claim that sat on the top of a ridge above the Haggarty Creek, two miles downstream from Dillon. It was only about ten acres of land in all. He spent one summer building a small cabin for himself before he'd met and married Hannah's mother.

The cabin was an A-frame, its steep roof protecting the structure from the weight of the deep winter snows. If anywhere in the world was home to Hannah, this rough little cottage was it. As she sat at Bridger Peak, she could picture the cabin that awaited her arrival. Inside the front door were the stairs to the loft, her small, but cozy bedroom. There was only room for Dad to stand up in the very middle, but Hannah, that first summer at least, could walk around the bed and get to the small dresser on one side and the table on the other. The bed had a wooden headboard that her father made himself; the deep blue quilt was stitched by his mother. Downstairs to Hannah's right was a door to the small coat closet, to the left was a large common room that held a couch and chair and coffee table, a built in bookshelf full of books and games, and a small kitchen in the far corner with a table for four. Under the staircase in the dining area was another door which led to the room her father used both as his bedroom and study.

From the first time she saw it, Hannah loved the cabin. It felt like a doll house, or perhaps one of the cottages in fairy tales that housed a princess before she knew she was actually a princess.

"Daddy, why haven't I ever been here before?" Hannah asked in awe.

"It is a lot of trouble to bring a baby or a toddler here. Your mom worried so much about your safety. She prefers family vacations which include room service instead of bugs and an outdoor toilet." They both laughed at that.

Hannah smiled now at the memory. She and her mother had always been close, and still were. The cabin became a special bond between Dad and Hannah, and gave her mom a little time to herself, so everyone was happy. The family also continued to take the kind of vacations her mom enjoyed as well, visiting the Grand Canyon one year, Disneyland another. Hannah enjoyed those times, but treasured the trips to the cabin.

The day they'd arrived each year at the cabin, there was much to do. They had to hang out all the bedding to get the dust out. They chopped wood for the fire: Hannah carried and helped stack while Dad ran the chainsaw and used the ax to split the logs. They walked down to the creek and carried water. "Hannah, it isn't safe for us to drink this water straight out of the creek. In the old days, people were used to the germs that may be in this water, but we are too used to chlorine and sterile lives. You saw the water jugs I filled before we left home, those are what we'll drink and cook with. This water we'll boil on the stove and use to wash dishes and take baths in, okay?"

Hannah agreed. Everything was such an adventure. They made a fire outside and cooked hamburgers on a grate over it. She couldn't remember a hamburger that ever tasted so good before or since that one. They sat outside for a long time that evening watching the campfire. Hannah listened again to stories of Dillon and the Rudefeha mine. Dad told her about the tram they built to carry the copper to Encampment. She could almost hear the squeak of the pulleys and groans of the cables taking the buckets of ore to town. She watched the coals in the campfire and listened and imagined.

Just as she was about to be lulled to sleep, Hannah and Dad heard a noise that made the hairs on her arms and neck stand up. At first Hannah thought someone had screamed, but knew no one was around. She found herself in her father's arms, sitting on his lap.

"Hannah, don't be afraid, that's just the old mountain lion welcoming you to her land. She isn't too far away, and she's noticed we're here. This land belongs to us according to some paper men made up, but really, this mountain belongs to that mountain lion, and it always will. She lives not too far from here, I'll show you the area, but you don't need to be afraid of her. She'd rather eat a deer than a little girl and her dad. She just wants us to know that she's here. She wants us to know that we're here as her guest."

"Have you ever seen her, Daddy?"

"No, I never have. I have heard her lots of times, and I've seen her tracks and sometimes the tracks of her young, but I haven't ever seen her."

"How do you know it's a girl?"

"Well, the girls have to settle down and take care of their young. The boy lions roam around and travel a long way, visiting their families and seeing what there is to see. Since I know that this one has a den, I know it's a mama."

***

Sitting on Bridger Peak remembering that conversation reminded Hannah of all the ways her father explained things. He could handle the most difficult or sensitive subjects with the most clear and simple explanations. "Dad, I hate being on this peak alone," she said aloud to the wind and the vista around her. Tears were instantly threatening her. She pushed the tears away and thought instead of the irony of her statement. She was indeed alone on Bridger Peak, but she was also alone and felt stranded on a lonely mountain in her life as well. Her father was gone. He'd died two months before. She'd always relied on him to listen to her troubles and help her solve them using his wisdom and his sweet explanations. Now he was gone and couldn't explain to her how to go on without him, or what to do about Greg, or to comfort her and encourage her about her job.

"It is all so unfair," Hannah said to the rocks and trees nearby. "How can you be gone when I need you more now than ever?"

Hannah wasn't naturally a bitter person, but regret and anger and frustration crowded out her normal optimism and she felt hopeless and negative. Losing Dad was the last straw.

Finally, Hannah stretched and stood up. She looked around her at the grand view once more and then began the hike back to her car. It was easier going downhill, and she was at her little car in no time. The trees were close enough to the road that turning the Cavalier around involved see-sawing back and forth across the road, carefully backing up and then cranking the steering wheel to inch forward several times before she was headed down the trail to the highway. At the junction with the highway, she turned right into the valley. She could see Battle Lake at times through the trees and smiled at its serenity. She adored the small lake that nestled into the bottom of a large bowl shaped mountainside.

***

"Back in 1904, a man who lived in this area thought he saw a lake serpent in Battle Lake," her father told her once when they were driving in.

"He claimed that he watched a huge snake-like creature swim across the top of the water of the lake. He described the monster as having a horn on its head, and told a reporter for the Dillon newspaper that he watched the serpent stab his horn through a horse that was tied up near the lake and take him into the water."

"Dad, are you making that up?" twelve year old Hannah asked him, laughing.

"No, Girl, I read about it in the *DoubleJack*. The story was printed on the front page."

"Do you think it is true?"

"What do you think about it?" he returned, challenging her to think it through for herself.

"Maybe he saw something and his imagination got the better of him," she answered. "I'm not sure I'd believe that little lake could hold anything big enough to take down a horse."

Later that trip they filled their day packs with water, cinnamon bears and snacks and walked into Battle Lake to see for themselves. Hannah lost herself in the peace and quiet serenity of the lake while also keeping a sharp eye out for horse-eating serpents. While they sat on the bank, her father told her a more believable story about Thomas Edison.

"Edison came west with a group of astronomers in 1878. A man named Henry Draper was a pioneer in taking pictures of the heavens, and he brought a group out here to see and photograph a total eclipse of the sun. Edison was in the group. People say that he came to Battle Lake and did some fishing. While he was here, someone knocked a bamboo fishing pole into the campfire. Afterwards, when Edison sat waiting for a fish to bite, he didn't see any monsters, but he studied the inside of that burnt fishing pole and had an idea about how to make an invention he was thinking about actually work. He went home from that trip, put his idea to use and created the first incandescent light bulb."

Hannah considered how easy it would be to sit at this lake and think of nothing and was even more impressed that Edison sat in this peace and thought of something that benefitted the whole world.

It was more fun, though, to think about water monsters, so she tied a cinnamon bear to the end of an old fishing line she'd found wrapped in a tree, and threw it in the water. Her father laughed his melodic, happy laugh then, and she knew he wasn't making fun of her, but enjoying her and the moment.

***

"That's something I learned from him that I haven't practiced in a while," she thought to herself as she rounded the last bend before the turnoff to the cabin. "Dad always was able to enjoy life moment by moment. He worried the least of any person I have ever known."

The turnoff came into sight, and her heart sped up a little, as it always did at this turn. She thought about the last time she'd been at the cabin. She'd just graduated from high school and was a bit petulant. She wanted to be with her Dad at the cabin, but the world beyond her home was beckoning and she couldn't relax and enjoy the time. She was short with her father several times on the trip, and realized now that she probably hurt his feelings by wanting to leave early. She understood now that Dad recognized that would be their last trip together since she was going away to college. It made her sad to know she behaved badly, short-sighted and selfish.

The cabin came into sight. It looked just as it always did - the one port in the storm of her life that never changed. She pulled up in front of the cabin and turned the car off. A palpable wave of grief hit her like it was a north wind. Her eyes burned and filled with tears. She hugged the steering wheel, put her head on her arms and sobbed for a few minutes. She'd never been here without him before and she felt his absence now in a deeper and more primal way than she ever had, even at the funeral. She considered starting the car and leaving again, the pain was so intense. In the end, she took a breath, took off her watch and put it in the glove box, and went in.

Opening the front door, tears welled up again. She closed and leaned against it, absorbing the welcome along with the silence. After a moment her tears were in check. Once she was inside and going through the routine of readying the cabin for a visit, she relaxed some. She carried the quilt from the bed in the loft outside and hung it up on the line to air out. Retrieving the sheets from a box she'd carried from the trunk of her car, she made the bed and dusted the furniture upstairs and down. She brushed the spider webs from the windowsills and opened the outside shutters so that the late afternoon light poured into the little cabin, warming the cool air and her heart. The door to Dad's bedroom and study was closed when she entered the cabin, as usual. After tidying up the kitchen and washing down the counters, Hannah stopped and stared at the door. She knew she needed to go in there and eventually make it hers instead of some sort of shrine to her dad. *Not yet*, she thought, and turned away.

She only brought with her the bare essentials for one night. She unpacked them from the second box she'd retrieved from the trunk. She sat the bottled water and juice on the little counter and stored the box of granola bars and bag of raisins inside the cupboard. She put the can of Dinty Moore stew and the package of crackers on the counter for her dinner later.

Hannah found the bucket just where her dad always left it and walked to the creek to fill it. She carried it back to the cabin and poured the water into the big pot they always used for heating creek water. She had never lit the fire before by herself, but there was plenty of wood stacked out on the porch and a pile of newspaper and a basket of kindling beside the stove. It took her a few tries to get the paper and kindling situated just right, but soon a fire danced nicely in the stove and the water began to warm. There was a small oak table along with two chairs stored up next to the bookshelf. She carried them out to their rightful place on the porch. The last job she did was to remove the binding from the porch swing so that it could swing freely.

Hannah sat back and looked around her. She remembered sometimes being impatient with her father on the day they were leaving, because he insisted on cutting and stacking wood outside to replace any they'd used. He always made sure that the kindling basket was full and that everything was ready for the moment they returned. She silently thanked him for making sure she was well taken care of, even now, and vowed that she would always leave the cabin ready for her return. She was also thankful that he had left her the cabin. All hers. She knew that monetarily, it wasn't an amazing inheritance, but to her it was priceless. She thought about how wonderful it would be to bring her own children here someday. With that thought, the debacle of Greg and the end of their relationship threatened to take over her homecoming. She snapped that door in her brain closed tightly and got up.

She knew Dad visited the cabin without her several times in the past few years. Five summers he'd called and asked her if she could make time for a few days, and five summers she'd been too busy with college, then grad school and internships, and last year with her new 'important job' to be able to come. She wished that she had rearranged her priorities in some of those years, but made herself stop thinking about those regrets, too.

Hannah took a short walk, smiling at the memories that crowded by every tree and rock. She'd sat on that rock and finally won the watermelon seed spitting contest against Dad. They built a swing in that tree with a rope and a length of two by four. She could see his face when the limb gave way and her dad toppled to the ground after they'd worked so hard to get the rope up there. They'd laughed and laughed that evening.

She sat on the porch and remembered all the games they'd played at the small oak table. She loved playing Scrabble and cribbage with Dad, and while he never let her win, he coached her so that even when she was young, she won fair and square some of the time.

Hannah warmed up the canned stew and ate it with crackers crunched up in the bowl while she sat on the porch swing. The altitude of the mountains made the evening get cold as soon as the sun went below the crest of the western mountains, so she went inside then. She took the propane lantern with her and prepared for bed.

As she settled into her bed in the loft, she looked at the Bible sitting on the table. She thought about the Bible stories her dad talked with her about, about his deep faith, and about the way they prayed together each night before bed in this cabin. Hannah felt alone and abandoned. Her dad was gone, Greg was gone. She looked at the Bible and wondered where God was. She wasn't really mad at God, she simply felt far away from Him. She left the Bible where it was and snuggled into bed. She reached over and turned off the lantern, and welcomed the deep, rich blackness of the night. Nowhere else was as dark as the cabin at night. She mused about how she was never frightened at night up here, feeling instead safe and secure in the encompassing darkness.

Chapter 3

June 18, 1902

Surprisingly, Andriette slept well and woke up refreshed. She spent some time in prayer. By the time she was dressed and came downstairs, she felt confident and ready. Nathan was in the lobby. He had a cup of coffee in hand and looked flushed and perhaps feverish.

"Are you feeling alright?" she asked as they sat down to breakfast. "You look a little peaked."

He looked sheepish and gave her a small, crooked smile. "I didn't sleep very well last night, I, well, I. Today is going to be a big day, and." He stopped and looked at her. She saw embarrassment and fear.

"Nathan, if you are unsure, then we can wait. If you don't think I am who you thought I was in my letters, then I'll understand and I will get back on the train this morning." Now her fears were rising.

"No!" His voice was a little louder than he intended, and people at tables near them looked up. "Good Grief, Andriette, that isn't the problem at all. I think you are wonderful and I am sure of our decision, I'm just as nervous as I can be."

She smiled then and took his hand across the table. They didn't speak again for a minute or two while the connection and warmth of her hand on his icy one calmed them both. He took a breath and tried to smile. "Andriette, you are so pretty and you seem close to perfect to me. I have been awake all night thinking about our life in the mountains, and it isn't much. The cabin I've built is small and rough, and the winters are hard like nothing you've ever seen. I don't have much to offer you."

These were words she had read in his letters. He was very honest with her about what his life was like. She wasn't surprised and she wasn't afraid. "Nathan, all I am offering you is myself, my companionship and loyalty. I promise to work hard beside you and be your partner. I promise to care for you and fight with you and laugh with you. So you see, I have even less to offer than you have."

He stared at her for a long moment, absorbing her words and the look on her face. Then he took a deep breath and knew what she said was true. "Let's go to the courthouse."

***

Rawlins lies on the main Union Pacific Railroad track which runs east and west. By the time the builders of the railroad reached Rawlins in 1886, they knew that they were in a race with the Central Pacific to lay the most miles of track. The Red Desert around Rawlins is flat and desolate. Its rough hide is covered in sagebrush and snakes, wild ponies and antelope. On summer days like today, they could see for fifty miles across the desert floor and into the foothills. The Desert is surrounded by mountains: the Sierra Madres jutting up to meet the tall billowing thunderheads to the south, and the Seminoes reaching skyward in the east.

Nathan and Andriette were on the trail by eleven o'clock. Nathan's rig was a large buckboard wagon filled with supplies to help them survive the winter. The load was covered with a thick canvas, tied down neatly and securely. Two Morgan horses pulled the buckboard, and a third Morgan followed, tied at the back of the wagon. To make Andriette more comfortable, Nathan added a cushion on the seat. They followed a dirt track that took them south and a bit east.

Nathan explained to her that they would make about fifteen miles before they'd need to camp out for the night. Today they needed to go over Nevin Ridge, which was a difficult area most of the year due to the limitless wind.

"I could have met you at Walcott station, and you could have had a shorter day yesterday on the train." Nathan began.

"I remember Walcott. When we left Medicine Bow I didn't know there was another stop before Rawlins, so at first I thought we were coming into Rawlins as the train slowed. It looked so small and uninviting."

"It is small, just a station where the steam engines fill up with water. There isn't a hotel or café there like in Rawlins." He looked at her a bit shyly. "Rawlins is the county seat. Walcott doesn't have a justice of the peace." He smiled shyly at her from under his hat and took her hand. They continued in silence for a while.

"Tomorrow's trip will be long, but flat. We'll get an early start in the morning and cover the next thirty five miles to Encampment. My mother lives in Encampment. We'll stay with her and have a good rest after a hard day. Out of Encampment, the trip will get interesting because we'll be out of the flats and the sagebrush and into the mountains."

The day was warm, but not too hot. As they reached Nevin Ridge the wind picked up, carrying fine sand that irritated her eyes. Andriette was glad when they turned a bit more southward and the wind decreased. They spent the time talking and getting comfortable with each other. They both found that they really did know each other well through the letters they'd written all those months. Frequently through the first afternoon, Andriette looked down at her left hand to gaze at the new ring there. She had not expected him to have a wedding ring for her. He told her over and over in his letters how careful he needed to be to live, and she knew him to be a plain and practical man. When the judge asked if they had a ring, she shook her head no even as she watched Nathan reach into his vest pocket and produce one. She studied it as they rode. It was a very simple, wide gold band.

It fit her perfectly and looked natural on her hand. Once, she looked up to find Nathan watching her. He put his arm around her then.

The sun was close to the western horizon when Nathan found a nice spot in a small arroyo near some scrub trees and a small creek. The grass under the trees was thick and soft, the creek chattered happily as it tumbled over its rocky bed. Andriette was happy to be off the buckboard. She helped Nathan gather dried sage branches, becoming more nervous with every twig she picked up. It was her wedding night and she did not know what to expect. She wasn't an ignorant little girl. Nathan was, in fact, her husband. Their correspondence spanned over two years. Yet, the idea of consummating their marriage on a bed roll out in the open when she had only been with him a day made her stomach tie up in knots. Nathan got more and more quiet as well.

As the light was fading and they both picked at the dinner he warmed over the campfire, the tension between them grew unbearable. Nathan stood up and walked over to her. He reached for her hand and helped her stand up. Then, he took her in his arms for the first time and held her. Andriette began telling herself silently *He is my husband. It is his right to do what he wants.*

Nathan spoke then, quietly. "Andriette, you are my wife and you are very lovely. I want you to be my wife in every way, but I want us both to be ready. Would it be alright with you if I held you tonight and that's all? We'll both know when it is right to go any farther."

At first he didn't understand the tears on her cheeks when he raised her face to look at her. He thought perhaps she was disappointed in his decision to wait, until he saw the tension leave her face and felt her arms tighten around him. "I'd like that," was all she said, but it was enough for him to understand that his decision was right.

They got ready and lay down beneath the wagon on the bed he fashioned for them. Off in the distance they could hear a coyote howling. "Dear Lord," Nathan said quietly out loud. "Thank you for bringing us safely this far. Thank you for Andriette and for our marriage this morning. I pray that we honor you with our lives together and how we treat one another. Lord, please see to it that we make it safely to Encampment tomorrow. In Jesus' name, Amen."

Chapter 4

August 18, 2007

Hannah slept well in the safe comfort of the familiar cabin. She loved how the darkness wrapped her in its soft blanket. She loved the silence of the night forest. She slept soundly until the sun began to show itself in the mountains by turning the sky first a dusty blue and then a muted pink. She lay in bed for a while, not moving, only feeling and being. It was strange to be all alone in the cabin. She missed the early morning sounds of her father waking and starting the fire in the stove to make coffee. Dad had been gone for two months. In that time she'd achieved an uneasy peace about his death – she accepted it as reality – but she railed internally at the injustice of it. Maybe he was ready to go, but she wasn't ready to be left.

When she tried to talk to her mom about her feelings in a phone call two weeks ago, the conversation turned sour.

"Mom, how could you support Dad in his decision not to have more radiation or chemo treatments? It was a death sentence for him." She tried to keep the accusing tone from her voice, and hoped she was succeeding.

"It was what he wanted. He tried the radiation and it hadn't been very effective, even the doctors weren't recommending more. While the chemo was more effective the first time, it made him so sick and weak. The doctors only gave him a 50-50 chance of increasing his life for more than a year or two with the chemo. Hannah, we talked and talked about all the options before he came to his decision. I had to respect it and support him."

"You could have insisted. He would have done it if you asked him to, he loved you so much!"

"Yes, he did," was Mom's quiet answer. "And I loved him enough to understand that he wanted his last weeks to be on his own terms. Darling, I love you. I am really sorry you are hurting so badly. I am praying for you – that you'll find peace and acceptance in all this. "

"It's really hard to accept what didn't have to be." She ended the conversation quickly then, trying to be more upbeat and nice, but seething at her mom.

Hannah knew she had been unfair. It was beyond her that Mom couldn't see just how unfairly Dad acted in deciding not to fight the cancer in his body. She needed him around, didn't he know that?

Taking a breath, she snuggled deeper into the muslin sheets on her cabin bed. She was angry at her mom for supporting her dad, and she was mad at him for leaving her. Somewhere deeper inside, she was unforgiving of God for taking him as well. She replayed her mother's words and her own over and over in her mind. As the days since the conversation passed, she could hear the selfishness in her own point of view more and more, but was as yet unwilling to let go of it.

Hannah turned over and stretched. There was no clock on the small table beside her bed. That was one of many fun traditions that Dad had begun when he built the cabin. No clocks. When he arrived at the cabin and parked each year, watches went in the glove compartment of the car or truck, not to be seen again until they were on their way home. There were no clocks in the cabin at all. The sun was the only measure of time.

Hannah loved the tradition. After living at the mercy of clocks and school bells and appointment times, the respite from the demands of time was a refreshing part of the allure of the cabin. It was as if time didn't matter here. They ate when they were hungry, slept when tired. It wasn't just daily time that didn't matter here, either. The closeness of the ghost towns of Copperton, Dillon, and Rudefeha kept the history of the area alive in her mind. They had copies of the area's newspapers from the late 1800s and early 1900s in the cabin. In the morning, Dad drank coffee and read *The Dillon DoubleJack* and the *Encampment Echo.* Those, along with the stories her father told her about the people and events here gave Hannah the privilege of living not only in her own time, but in that other time as well.

Roger Harding, Hannah's father, was always a studious, quiet and gentle man. He loved his position as a history professor at the University of Nebraska in Omaha, and often preferred the company of the pioneers who explored and tamed the west more than he did that of his colleagues and neighbors. As a teen, Hannah read his books and was delighted that his writing style mirrored perfectly the voice he used to tell her stories about the past. As she grew, she realized that her father was a popular professor and author because of his ability to make people and events from long ago come alive to his students and readers.

When she was little, the ghosts of the people of Dillon were her playmates, not literally of course, but certainly in her vivid imagination. Imagining was easy while she played and explored around the foundations and falling walls of old cabins and buildings. On the first few trips they made to the mountains, many of the buildings around Dillon still had walls standing that were taller than Hannah. The roofs all were caved in, but the walls, along with pictures from the newspapers and other historical sources her dad accumulated, afforded her a clear enough picture of the main street of town that she knew where the boarding house and the bank were, along with the mercantile and the saloon. While her father poked around on his own, or sat on a rock nearby reading or writing, Hannah spent many hours every summer to herself in Dillon, playing and pretending that the town was alive and well and that she lived there.

***

Thirteen year old Hannah sat on a rock in front of a large foundation at the heart of what was once Dillon. Her father sat near her on a rock of his own. She considered life in the mountains, and how difficult things would be without modern conveniences.

"Dad, the road we come up here on is full of rocks. It isn't smooth, it crosses the creek twice."

Her father took his reading glasses off and put them in his pocket. He put the cap on his pen and looked up at Hannah. He waited for her to go on.

"Were the roads better back then? I mean, so that it was easier to travel up here?"

"Well, the road we come up to get here was one of two main roads they used. Our road, up Haggarty Creek and the road over the top that came by Bridger Peak probably were a bit better, in that they probably had a smoother layer of dirt and gravel on them than they do now. Through all the years, the dirt has eroded away and left the huge rocks that we have to contend with. The road wasn't any wider, and it crossed the creeks just like today. It wasn't an easy trek, and that has a lot to do with why the town died.

"In the winter, the Haggarty Gulch road was impassable, and only really hearty souls ventured to travel using the Peak road. The people made the trip using snowshoes. They even put snowshoes on the horses."

Hannah giggled at the idea of a horse wearing snowshoes. Serious again, Hannah continued. "How did they get all the mining equipment and supplies up here? I can visualize a wagon pulled by horses bringing up food and household things, but at the mine we see big heavy rails, and the ore cars that ran on them, and the big cables and all that. How did that stuff get up here?"

Dad smiled and got a twinkle in his eyes so that Hannah knew he was going to tell her a story. "The most famous driver in all this area was a man named Jack Fulkerson. He was an ornery fellow by all accounts I've read, but he was an amazing teamster. He hauled all kinds of supplies up to Dillon and Rudefeha using a large team of horses. He used between ten and sixteen horses or mules to pull a wagon, depending on the weight of it. He hauled all the cable for the tramway, about 17,000 pounds of it in one big coil, up to the mine using fifteen horses."

"How could he handle that many horses?"

"That's a good question. I did some research about that when I wrote that article about Dillon last year. Normally, a driver has in his hands two straps for each horse in the line, so with a fifteen horse or mule team, a driver could have up to thirty lines in his hands to control and hold. Fulkerson did it a different way. He must have been an amazing guy, and he must have been really good at training and controlling his animals, because he only used one line. He'd hold on to the line of the lead horse – this was called a jerk line – and control all the animals with just that one line. He also never sat on the wagon. Instead, he rode one of the back horses.

"My favorite story of Jack Fulkerson is that once he hauled a big load of dynamite up to the mine. He had been at it all day and he was tired and sore and hungry. He was a typical horseman, though, and he couldn't rest or eat until his load was off and he unhooked and tended to his horses. He arrived at the mine just at supper time. He walked in and told the clerk at the mine that he needed some help unloading the dynamite so that he could tend his horses and be done for the day. The clerk politely informed him that the miners were eating, and that they would help him after their dinner hour was over.

"Well, old Jack didn't like that answer at all, and his temper flared up. He walked right back out to his wagon and climbed up in it. He started shoving and kicking those boxes of dynamite right off the end of the wagon, cussing and hollering all the while. That sure got the attention of the miners at dinner in a hurry, and they came right out to help him finish unloading."

Hannah sat for a long time picturing the looks on the faces of the miners. They must have been afraid they were going to be blown up before they could calm Jack down enough to help him unload.

Chapter 5

June 19, 1902

The next morning brought a cloudless blue sky and a steady but gentle breeze. Early in the night Andriette got cold and moved closer to Nathan. He turned over when he felt her next to him and cuddled her close. She slept soundly then, warm and safe. She awoke to the sound of coffee percolating in a small pot at the edge of the fire. She turned over and sat up, hoping that her hair wasn't a complete wreck. Nathan smiled at her and asked how she was.

"I slept so well. I didn't expect to, really, I've never slept outside before."

Nathan chuckled. "When I was a boy, I slept outside in the summer more than inside. I love the stars over my head at night."

They ate a quick breakfast of coffee and bread they'd purchased in Rawlins, and climbed on the buckboard. As they had the day before, they chatted and talked. Every two hours Nathan stopped the rig so they could rest and walk around. Andriette was tired and sore from the constant bouncing of the wagon, but she didn't say anything about it to Nathan. During these breaks, Nathan unhooked one of the Morgans from the front of the wagon and replaced him with the one tied behind. "These three horses are all I have to help me make a living. I have to treat them kindly and make sure I don't wear them out. Pulling this load is hard work for them, so I like to rotate them and give each one a rest."

She watched how gently he treated the animals, and how carefully he looked at their hooves and legs before they started each time. *Lord, thank you for bringing this gentle man into my life.*

They were silent for a while after they were moving again when Nathan started to speak. "Andriette, I haven't ever told you much about my family. My letters to you were awfully self-centered, and I talked only about me."

She thought back on Nathan's letters. She would never have called them selfish. He described his solitary life as a woodsman; he told her about the mountains with such strong descriptions that she felt as if she had already seen them. He talked openly about his faith and his hopes for the future. In his letters, he was the main character and the only one she was interested in.

Nathan continued, "My father came west and brought my mother with him about thirty years ago. He worked for a while building the road that we will take into the mountains, but he hurt his back and couldn't do rough work anymore. That's when he and my mother opened a little hardware and tool store in Encampment and built a house there. My father was a good man, and he taught me how to be strong and to love hard work. He died about five years ago. My mother and sister are still in Encampment running the store. My sister, Abby, is married and has a young'un on the way. Her husband, Mark, works in the copper smelter in Encampment. We'll stop at my mother's house and spend the night. She and Abby are really anxious to meet you. You'll get to have a bath and a great meal and a good night's rest after this bouncing around in the dust for the past two days.

Andriette felt the muscles in her neck and shoulders tighten. Her own father and the two aunts who made up her family were so negative about her plans and so vocal about their distaste for the choice she was making, that her last few months at home in Council Bluffs were grueling. Her own family was never close knit. Perhaps if her mother had lived through Andriette's childhood, life would have been different. The fact was, Andriette's experience with family was not a good one. Her aunts raised her after her mother died, and they resented the added burden. They were petty and gossipy women. Her father was distant and impatient, and he didn't put much value in a girl child. She learned to be as invisible and as quiet as possible around them.

Andriette's mind was a jumble. Nathan was close to his family, and that made her afraid that her marriage could be doomed if Nathan's mother and sister didn't accept her and like her. She looked down at the dusty traveling dress she was wearing, knowing that her hair was a mess and her face was probably grimy, and she could not imagine how meeting Nathan's family could turn out any way but badly.

Nathan felt her tense up beside him. He put his arm around her and tried to reassure her. "My mom is a loving woman. While she hasn't actually read your letters to me, I have told her about you and she has been very supportive of our relationship. When I left Encampment five days ago, she and Abby were as excited as can be. They were cleaning the house and planning for your arrival. Don't you worry. They already love you."

Andriette heard his words but struggled to absorb them. Her own family wasn't very accepting, would these people accept her? *Oh God, what do you have in mind here? I am so scared that they won't like me, so Lord, please help me to say the right things and please soften their hearts so that they can accept me.* She continued to pray for several minutes as they bounced along.

Until mid-day, they stayed on the flats, and then an unbroken line of foothills began growing in the west. By the time the sun began its descent, the scenery started to change. Off to the left, the east, in the distance she could see a line of tall trees snaking through the middle of the valley where a river ran. The lush green of that crooked path was a stark contrast to the dusty, bluish green of the sagebrush and the brown of the dried grasses of the rolling prairie. Nathan told her it was the North Platte River, considered a large river for southern Wyoming, and important for its water to the valley farms.

The horizon to the east was blocked by mountains called the Snowy Range. The name was apt, since even in June the tops of the peaks were white with snow. They were heading west into the Sierra Madre Mountains. Since Nathan and Andriette were closer to this range, it was hard to tell that if these or the Snowys were taller. The peaks of the Sierras were snow covered as well. They drew ever closer to the Sierra Madre foothills as the afternoon wore on.

She was so lost in thought and prayer that it took a while for her to register what she was seeing. "Nathan," she finally broke the silence between them. "What is that coming off that hill?"

"Those are towers that will soon hold almost sixteen miles of cables and move big buckets down from the high mountains up there." He pointed off to their right.

"What is it for?"

"Up near the very top of this mountain range is a large copper mining operation. The mountains are so rugged and steep that it would be nearly impossible for the copper that they mine to be hauled out on wagons, so they are creating this tramway. It will carry the copper ore in buckets down to the smelter in Encampment where it will be melted down and turned into copper bricks for shipment to other places."

"It sounds impossible."

"It is indeed a great undertaking. They began building it in February and they already have thirty towers done. Just last week there was trouble up near Cow Creek. There was a small forest fire that ran them out, then they stirred up a couple bears that gave them fits for a day or two."

"How long will it take them to finish it?" Andriette asked, twisting in her seat to look at the line of towers marching off into the mountains.

"They hope to have it operating by next summer. How they are going to work all winter is beyond me, though."

Nathan shook his head. Then, motioning ahead he changed the subject. "That's Encampment up ahead, we're almost there."

The town was larger than she expected. It was nestled into a small, high bowl surrounded by sagebrush. At the east side of the bowl, lower than the west side, was a line of trees that heralded a river. Near the trees was a set of very large wooden buildings with two tall chimneys. This is where the line of towers began. Nathan pointed them out to her and explained that what she was seeing was the smelter complex. Houses and streets dotted the rest of the bowl. Towards the west side of the middle rested a line of larger buildings of brick and wood. This was clearly the downtown area of Encampment.

As they passed through downtown, Nathan pointed out his family's store and other wooden buildings. He greeted a few people on the street and returned waves from other wagons and people walking on the wooden board walk. They continued on, heading up towards the mountains and the outskirts of town. There stood a two story stone house in the middle of a trimmed, green lawn lined with manicured beds brimming with flowers. The house was grey cut stone with a nicely painted porch. Even before they arrived, two women stepped out on the porch and began waving. One, the elder, wore a plain blue dress with a tidy white apron. She looked like the pictures Andriette admired in magazines of the perfect home maker. The younger woman beside her resembled her mother, only slightly shorter with her hair pulled back gently into a braid. As she stepped off the porch and walked to greet them, the small but pronounced roundness of her tummy became noticeable.

"Good heavens, Nate, can you possibly make those horses walk any slower?" She scolded him with laughter in her voice. "This poor girl is probably tired beyond enduring, being in that seat with you. We've been watching for you for hours!"

Not waiting for introductions, as soon as Andriette was down off the buckboard, the younger woman grabbed Andriette into a strong and genuine hug. "Welcome! We're so glad you are here. I'm Nate's sister, Abby. Now maybe Nate will talk about something else instead of the latest news in one of your letters." Again, it was clear to Andriette that Abby was teasing. Nathan knew it too, but that didn't stop him from turning a bit red in the face. He hurriedly hugged his mother and then turned to introduce Andriette.

Andriette, now face to face with his mother, put out her hand, formally, and said, "It is so nice to meet you, Mrs. Jameson." The woman took her hand, and held it instead of shaking it. She closed her other hand over it and they stood looking one another. Andriette saw that Nathan had his mother's eyes. The kindness and warmth in them was unmistakable. "Welcome to our home and to our family, dear Andriette. I hope that you will come to think of us as your family and this as your home." She hugged her then, a real and heartfelt hug.

Andriette was overcome by the sweetness of the moment and struggled to find her voice. They stood and talked for several minutes. Nathan offered a bit of news from Rawlins, but most of the conversation was about Andriette's journey. Abby finally moved them by saying she needed to go in and check on supper. Mrs. Jameson gave Andriette a second hug as they started into the house. She broke the hug by holding Andriette by the shoulders at arm's length. "I'll bet you would like something to drink and time to clean up. Am I right?"

"Definitely both. I feel very much in need of a bath, if that would be ok?" she answered.

"Absolutely, we have water on and ready for you. Nathan," Mrs. Jameson called as he was leading the horses into the barn out back. He turned to look at the three of them. "When you can, could you carry Andriette's bags in and put them in Abby's room, please?"

"I only need my satchel, please," Andriette clarified.

Nathan smiled. "Sure, Ma'am," was his answer.

Abby and Andriette followed Lillian Jameson into the house. She gave a short tour then they moved towards the stairs. Andriette loved how light and airy the house was. Her father's home in Council Bluffs was paneled in dark woods; the windows draped with thick, dusky colored brocade. Those rooms were furnished with large pieces that always seemed overbearing and austere. This house was the opposite. The windows were covered with white lace which let in light and cheer. The furniture was all made of knotty pine, the walls either painted white or covered with wallpaper of small multicolored flowers. Everywhere she looked, there were cut flowers in vases. The house was clean and neat, but not the intimidating fastidiousness of her aunts. There, she feared disturbing anything. Here, she felt as if she could relax. They walked up the staircase as Mrs. Jameson explained that Nathan's father built the house and most of the furniture himself. "He was a skilled craftsman with wood," she said, with a nostalgic smile.

"We decided to put you in Abby's old room. Nathan's old room is right next door. You can decide where exactly you two will sleep." Said by anyone else, this may have embarrassed Andriette, but there was no mistaking that her words were meant to let Andriette know that she understood and wanted to make things as simple as possible. Again, Andriette had trouble finding her voice. She tried twice before actually making a sound.

"Thank you so much, Mrs. Jameson. I can't tell you how much your welcome has meant to me."

"One more thing, Dear. Please, I'd love it if you would call me Lillian."

This time her voice was more sure, "I'd be honored, Lillian, and thank you." They hugged again, and were just stepping apart as Nathan got to the top of the stairs with her satchel and pocketbook. "Is this all you need?" he asked.

"Thanks, Nathan, yes it is." Their eyes met for just a second, but in that time they connected. His eyes asked her if all was well, and she could tell that her return look assured him that it was. She took time to think about it later, and was amazed that while they had only known each other such a short time, the connection between them seemed strong.

"Nathan, there are two pots of water simmering on the stove, could you carry them up for us please?" Lillian smiled at Nathan.

"Yes, Ma'am," was his answer and he was gone.

The bedroom they showed her to was a corner room at the front of the house. There were windows towards the west and the north. The view out the north window was of the way they had just travelled, and she could see the mountains and the tram towers in the distance. The sun was near the horizon, but not yet down behind the mountains, and the room was bathed in golden light. The comforter on the large four poster bed was yellow, matching the yellow roses in the wallpaper. There were real roses in a vase on the table beside the bed, making the room smell sweet. In one corner was a deep, claw-footed bathtub with a straight backed wooden chair next to it piled with fluffy, white towels.

Andriette gasped, "This is such a beautiful room. But you have gone to so much work for me, having to haul water upstairs and then down again."

Abby laughed, "Yes, we do have to carry the water upstairs, but we won't have to carry it down. When I lived here, Papa and Nathan got tired of carrying water both ways for me, I love to take baths. So, instead, Papa created a drain for this tub. It goes outside and hooks into the storm drain from the roof. All you have to do is pull the plug and this bathwater will water Mom's roses!"

Andriette could tell how proud of her father Abby was, and once again compared this family to her own. Her father would never have agreed to carry water for her, or bothered himself with accommodating such a 'girlish' need.

Nathan arrived just then with a pot of steaming water in each hand. He poured them both into the tub and retreated quietly. Abby and Lillian took their leave as well, telling Andriette to take her time and relax. Dinner would not be ready for an hour or more.

Andriette first unbuttoned her dress and carefully slipped it off. It was so dusty from the trip that she was afraid it would leave dust on the chair she draped it over. She needed to remember to take it outside and shake it before they left in the morning to freshen it up. Dressed only in her thin cotton and lace camisole and petticoat, she opened her satchel and pulled out the dress carefully folded and packed at the bottom. It was the dress she originally intended to wear as her wedding dress, but when the plans were made and included leaving Rawlins as soon as the ceremony was over, she opted for wearing her travelling dress instead. She shook out the folds, and inspected the dress. It was white cotton with a pale green sash that tied at the back at her waist. It took her many hours to embroider a line of vines and small flowers along the neckline and hem of the dress. It didn't look too bedraggled after having been at the bottom of her satchel for so long, and she felt good about how she would look tonight for dinner. She found her aunts' necklace and laid it out as well. Then, she let her hair down out of the bun she had twisted it into this morning. She decided she wouldn't wash her hair now, it was so thick it would take an hour to dry. She planned to pin her hair up in a Gibson Girl bun for the evening. Charles Dana Gibson's drawing of the 'perfect American girl" appeared in *Life Magazine* recently and Andriette thought it would look good with her dress. She bent at the waist and flipped her hair over, brushing it to get out the dust and to put a little life back into it.

Just as she was flipping her hair back and standing up, the door opened and Nathan came in carrying another bucket of water. She stood up quickly, looking around. There was nothing near her to grab and cover herself with. Nathan nearly dropped the bucket, and stood staring. He stammered,

"I … I heard voices in Mother's room, so I thought you three were in there. I brought you some cool water in case the tub was too hot." As he spoke, his eyes travelled from her head to her toes. He was embarrassed but at the same time intrigued. At first she was mortified to be seen in her petticoat by a man, then it occurred to her that this was her husband. She could have reacted many ways, but what she did surprised them both, she giggled.

"Thank you, Husband, for the water." She said it with humor and seriousness, and he understood exactly what she meant. He sat the bucket beside the tub and turned, letting his eyes travel over her once more. What she saw there was approval and something more.

"Thank *you*, Wife," was all he said as he left the room.

Chapter 6

August 18, 2007

Hannah lazed around the cabin, drinking coffee and listening to the mountain sounds. She loved to hear the wind rustle the tops of the lodge pole pines high above her. She boiled some water and sugar and after it cooled, she filled the hummingbird feeder and hung it on the hook at the end of the porch. Within just a few minutes she was smiling at the antics of three tiny birds dive-bombing each other and fighting over the sweet treat.

The August sun was warm and bright, and Hannah felt stronger and more peaceful as the quiet morning drew on. Finally, she put a cooler in the trunk of her car and gathered her keys. Since her vacation was a week long, she'd planned to spend five nights at the cabin. She'd only brought supplies for one night though, because she knew she could run into Encampment and buy groceries.

Hannah stopped at the gate, making sure she locked it behind her as she left. Trespassers had never been a problem for them, but there were more and more people in these woods all the time. The drive into Encampment took about forty minutes. During the drive she watched for wildlife in the meadows she passed, but saw only wild flowers. She loved coming to the cabin in August in large part because the flowers bloomed then, and she hoped that the wild strawberries and raspberries would be ripe as well.

She pulled up in Encampment at the small local grocery. She sat in the car for a minute considering the building that housed the grocery. This building, built in 1904, was one of the oldest in town. It had been the main offices for the North American Copper Company at first. Later, the building housed the bank. This old brick building stood as witness to the rise and fall of the copper boom and the changes in the whole area. In the nineteen fifties, the building stood silently as most of the rest of the businesses on Main Street burned down, its brick protecting it so it could continue into a new century, standing and watching the waxing and waning of the town.

Hannah got out and crossed the street. She walked through the small store, picking out what she'd need for the week. She took time to look at the old pictures on the walls, pictures that chronicled the years. There was a picture of this room when it was the bank. Prominent on the wall opposite where she was standing was the vault with its shiny black door decorated with gold lettering. There were tintypes of stage coaches filled with people stopped out front, and those of the tram line entering town not far from this spot. She loved the picture of the tram, showing an ore bucket gliding into town carrying not only the ore from the mine, but a man as well. "How often," she wondered, "have I looked at this picture and wished I could have done that?"

Bob Warren, the owner of the store, came out from the old bank vault with a stack of paper sacks in his hands. They used the space now for storage instead of holding the payroll for the smelter. Hannah had met Mr. Warren many times, and her father and he often enjoyed long conversations about the history of the area. She looked around, and sure enough, several copies of her father's books were displayed for sale on a nearby shelf. She wondered if he'd recognize her since it had been so long since she was last here. He greeted her cordially, and she assumed that his friendliness was generic, a habit most people in small Wyoming towns grew up showing to the people who were passing through.

"I was sad to hear your Dad passed away." His voice was quiet and kind.

"Thank you," Hannah answered, surprised.

He smiled then. Normally Hannah was uncomfortable with sympathy, but his warm eyes were a kind welcome.

"It's good to see you again, Hannah. You graduated from college last year, didn't you?"

"Yes, sir," she acknowledged. "I work for a graphic design firm in Denver now."

"I heard all about that when your dad was up here last. He surely was proud of you."

As he spoke, Bob rang up her groceries. Hannah busied herself with paying him, and didn't answer. She was glad for the diversion when another shopper arrived. Both Hannah and the grocer looked up as the door opened. A scruffy man, probably in his early thirties, came in. In Omaha, a man dressed rough and looking scraggly would have gotten ill looks and aroused suspicion, but here, where ranchers and farmers stopped in town in the midst of a hard day of work, no one thought twice about his appearance. The grocer said howdy, and the man answered quietly and walked to the back of the store.

"Are you headed up to the hills?" Bob asked her.

Hannah gathered up her bags and answered, "Yeah, five days of peace and quiet." They ended with kind farewells, and she headed out the door. She popped the trunk on her car and put the cold food into the cooler she'd brought with her. She went back across the street to the ice machine in front of the store to retrieve the bags of ice she'd bought, and carried them out to the car. She ripped open the ice bags and filled the cooler. She rumpled up the empty bags and stuffed them between the cooler and the side of the trunk and slammed it down. She did all this without thinking, just doing. She realized as she was starting the car that the tension in her neck and shoulders was waning, and she was starting to feel relaxed and ready for the next few days of not seeing another human being and being alone at the cabin.

Meanwhile, inside the store, the grocer's wife came from the back room. "That young woman looked familiar," she said to her husband.

"That was Roger Harding's daughter Hannah," answered the man. "She's sure grown up a lot since I saw her last, and she sure is stunning."

"Didn't we hear that Roger passed away?"

"Yeah, sad thing. Hannah is up for a few days to stay at the cabin."

"I didn't see anyone with her."

"No, it looked like she bought groceries for only one."

"I hope she does okay up there by herself."

He delayed responding to his wife while he rang up and began bagging the few groceries the stranger brought to the counter. "I imagine coming back to the cabin alone after all those years with her dad is hard on her. I expect we'll see her on her way out of the mountains. She and Roger always stopped to say goodbye and buy ice cream bars."

"The weather is supposed to be warm this week, I hope she has a nice and not too lonely visit," concluded his wife.

"I reckon she will. Haggarty Creek Gulch is so calm this time of year, before the hunters arrive and liven everything up."

The grocer smiled at his customer and handed him his grocery bag. "Thank you for coming in."

The man mumbled a quiet thanks and left the store. He walked down the street and got into an old, dusty green Ford pick-up truck.

Chapter 7

June 20, 1902

Andriette slept very well in Abby's bed with Nathan right next door, and they awoke early. Lillian prepared a huge and filling breakfast of pancakes and bacon, served with syrup and homemade jellies. The meal was pleasant and relaxed.

"Abby would have liked to come by and see you off this morning, but mornings are still hard for her with the baby coming." Lillian explained at the end of breakfast.

"She told us that before she left last night." Nathan assured her. He turned to Andriette, "I often make it all the way home from here, but the wagon is loaded heavy, so I am thinking we'll have to stay in Battle tonight."

"There's another town nearer to the cabin?" asked Andriette.

"There are actually a series of towns between here and the mine. Most of them are small, but each fills a need. We'll probably stay in Battle, at the boarding house there. It isn't a fancy place, mostly miners and travelers use it, but it is clean and the food is hearty. Then, where we turn off to go up the creek to our cabin, we'll be near Copperton. It is much smaller than the rest, mostly just a way station."

"Nathan, since you are stopping in Battle, would you take Pearl some jam for me?"

"Sure, Mom, we have room for jam."

He finished his coffee and got up to go ready the horses. Andriette began picking dishes up from the table. Lillian busied herself at the sink. When the table was clear, Andriette came to the sink to help wash or dry, but Lillian stopped her. She turned to face the younger woman, "Andriette, you are lovely, and I am very thankful for you. I worry so much about Nathan being up in those mountains all alone for so long. It will be wonderful for him to have a partner and a wife."

Lillian's voice was soft yet strong. Her eyes met Andriette's and held her in a circle of love and trust. Then she continued, "Nathan can be very driven, and he gets tunnel vision when he has a job in front of him. Don't you let him ignore you or take you for granted."

"No, I won't," but there was little conviction behind her answer. She always retreated when her father ignored her. She hoped she could stand up for herself and not become inconsequential in her new life. Untried as she was, she wasn't sure of the strength of her resolve.

"And dear Andriette, don't let yourself get too lonely. Lord knows, I couldn't live up there so far away from people, so I want you to be sure and take care of yourself. Nathan is a solitary man, he doesn't seem to need to be around people as much as I do. If you start getting lonely, you can always come here for a break. I'd love to have you." She hugged Andriette then, tightly.

They could hear the wagon and horses pull up in front. Lillian picked up a package from the counter and the two women stepped out on the porch.

"Your chariot awaits, Milady," Nathan smiled and doffed his hat to Andriette. He jumped down off the wagon to take the package from his mother and help his wife into the seat. He hugged Lillian.

"Nathan, you take good care of her," she scolded. "My offer still stands, when the snow starts, I really could use your help down here. Please consider it."

"I will," was his answer.

The road out of Encampment was a steady climb through the last of the sagebrush and scrub pine. The day was already hot, though the sun was barely above the horizon. Within two hours, the trees began, first mostly birch and aspen stands, and then into heavy pines. Soon they were in more heavy timber, and came to a small settlement. "This is Elwood. The post office here opened in 1900. The town isn't much, just about a hundred people, but it's important as a freight station. All the supplies for the mine and the towns above go through here. When the snow gets deep, freighters change from a wagon to a sled starting here, so that goods can make it up to the mines."

They stopped for a short rest while Nathan changed out the horses and talked with the liveryman. While they worked and talked, Andriette walked around. Through the trees she could see the valley between the mountain ranges. Large clouds billowed atop the Snowy Range peaks. When they were ready, Nathan helped her up and they got on their way. Immediately, the trees filtered out much of the sun, and Andriette reached under the seat for the sweater in her satchel.

They spoke only a little. Both of them were lost in their own thoughts. Nathan spent a bit of time remembering his encounter with Andriette before her bath. His pulse sped up at the thought of her long hair, tousled and cascading down her back. He saw again the beautiful outline of her slender body as she'd stood there, a little shy but not embarrassed. The look in her eye when she giggled assured him of the joy their marriage would bring him. His thoughts turned also to how lovely she looked at dinner. He'd loved the dress she wore. It flattered her in every way. He thought about how she'd laughed at a small joke he'd made. *She has a great laugh*, he thought. He marveled that such a lovely woman was sitting beside him, with his calloused hands and simple life. What he offered her wasn't a prize by the world's standards, and he couldn't help feel as if he didn't deserve her. Maybe more accurately, she didn't deserve what little he offered her.

He admired her quiet courage. She'd never name it that, but in the past three days he'd learned a little about how strong she was. She'd not complained even once about the dusty, rough trip. She was so quick to smile, even when she was tired and sore. Both his mother and Abby were much taken with Andriette, and for that he was very thankful.

He was so caught up in thinking about his bride that he was surprised to see they were in the trees when Andriette reached for her wrap.

Andriette's thoughts also started on dinner last night, and she prayed with thanks that the meeting with his family had gone so well. Dinner was very tasty, Lillian a wonderful cook. Abby's husband, Mark, came after he got off work, so the whole family gathered to enjoy an evening together. The conversation was comfortable. It was clear to Andriette that Mark and Abby's marriage was strong by the easy way they teased each other during the meal.

She could tell that his family's approval had been important to Nathan, and she truly felt welcomed and accepted. Her thoughts eventually turned, however, to what lay ahead of her. Nathan's letters described his life, and she was very aware that he lived in the mountains away from others. She looked forward to the solitary life he described. She loved being alone, and wasn't worried about the isolation. But Lillian's words had been so serious, that she turned her prayers to that topic. She prayed for a long while that God would grant her the ability to be the best wife she could for Nathan, and that loneliness would not be a problem for her. She felt better and more a peace when she ended her prayer time.

The road was steeper now, and it wound around through the trees. The road itself was surprisingly smooth, but the horses struggled with the incline and the altitude. As on the trip from Rawlins, they stopped to rotate the horses so they wouldn't tire as fast. As the mountain road became more steep, he rotated them about once every hour.

After one stop, Nathan got the horses moving again, then reached over and took her hand. "Andriette, thank you for being willing to take on this life with me. I am sure my mother said something to you about how lonely my life up here is."

She met his eyes and answered honestly that she had.

"She doesn't understand how I can love the mountains. She loves being around lots of people. She adores working in the store, because she can chat with people all day. I hope she didn't make you have second thoughts." Andriette could hear a big question mark lurking at the end of the sentence.

"Nathan, I am a little concerned about it, but I also know that I love to be on my own. I think that I will enjoy our life in the mountains, but I don't know for sure."

"Will you tell me how you are feeling? I want you to be happy there."

"Yes, I will talk to you. After I have talked to God about it, I will come to you."

"That's a deal." He smiled and relaxed.

"Nathan, what did Lillian mean about an offer?"

"For the last two years, I have stayed in the mountains for the winters. The snow gets really deep up that high, and it isn't always pleasant. After about the first of November, the only way to get around is with snowshoes. The storms and wind are horrific at times, and it is a hard life. I'm basically trapped up there. But, winter is beautiful, too. The storms have their own fierce glory, and the sun, while not warm, does come out between storms to reveal a new kind of world.

"Mother hates it that I stay up there. She worries about what would happen if I got sick or hurt and couldn't get down for help. Ever since I told her our plans for your arrival, she has been talking to me about coming down from the mountain before the snow gets too deep to travel. She would love for me to take over the store, and this is one way that she can see that happening."

"You don't want to, though."

"Someday I do imagine that I'll move down, I mean that maybe *we'll* move down, to Encampment permanently and take over the store when she gets older and can't run it on her own. Maybe it is selfish, but I do love the mountains and the work I do up there and the time I spend there. I really don't know what to do about this winter, though."

"Can I make a suggestion?"

"Andriette, I want your suggestions and ideas all the time. This isn't just my life now, it is ours." His words were so beautiful to her, no one ever cared what she thought or wanted before.

"How about we don't worry about making a decision now? It is the end of June. We have three months to get settled in together and then, when Fall arrives, we can make the decision together. If we both are praying about it, and both of us listen to the other, the decision should be easy to make."

The rest of the day passed easily. The horses would not have agreed, but for Nathan and Andriette, the day was one of calmness and beauty. Several times they saw deer feeding nearby. Many times they spooked quail and grouse up beside the road. Once, a little farther into the trees, there were two elk. Andriette had never seen an elk, and she was impressed with how regal they were with their tall antler crowns and the way they carried their heads high and proud.

Just at dusk, they reached the top of a ridge and entered the town of Battle. Nathan drove their rig past a saloon that announced itself as "Smizer's" with a sign above the door. They also passed The Battle Hotel and the Annex Chop House and Meat Market. Nathan turned onto a side street and followed it to the end. "This is the Battle Rooming House," Nathan turned in the seat and looked at his wife. "The hotels are lots fancier, but Mrs. Kinsella and my mother have been friends for years so I always stay here. Do you mind?" She could see in his eyes that if she asked to go to the hotel, he would take her.

"I think this will be just fine," she answered with a smile. Andriette was stiff and sore from the day's ride when Nathan helped her down. Nathan reached under the buckboard seat and retrieved the package Lillian had given them, handing it to Andriette. "Pearl works for Mrs. Kinsella running the boarding house, you will make points with her if you give her this," he said with a mischievous grin.

They walked in the door and were greeted by an enormous woman. She was taller than Nathan, and very round. Dressed in canvas trousers and a man's denim work shirt, she didn't appear fat, but instead heavy with large bones and developed muscles. Her voice was low and gruff, "It's about time you got home. I'd about given you up for a city slicker."

She came to greet them and enfolded Nathan in a bear hug. He made a hurried introduction, introducing Andriette as his wife. "What are you going to do with this little thing?" She turned to Andriette and swept her up into a bear hug as well. "Why she's too little to be much good at the saw mill, Nathan, what are you thinking?" She smiled and winked at Andriette.

"I'll find something she's good at," was his return.

Pearl winked again and snorted a laugh, "She sure is pretty, so I am sure you will!"

Andriette's face turned pink at Pearl's underlying meaning. In an effort to change the subject, Andriette handed the package to Pearl. "This is from Lillian," she managed to squeak out.

Pearl took the package as if it were worth a thousand dollars, "That Lillian makes the best jam around here. I'll bet this is rhubarb, it's too early in the year for raspberry."

Nathan stood next to Andriette. "Pearl, do you have a place for us to stay the night?"

"For you, anything. I only have two rooms in this boarding house to let, one for women and one for men, so you newlyweds will have to sleep apart tonight." Again, her words were innocent enough, but the tone underneath made

Andriette blush again. "You are in luck, though, because you are the only woman I have tonight. Nathan, you aren't as lucky, there are three miners on their way back up to Rudefeha bunking in with you."

"That'll be fine Pearl." He turned to Andriette, "Come with me to put the horses up, and then I'm sure Pearl will find something hot for us to eat."

"Got a meatloaf on and nearly ready. I'll dish it up by the time you get back."

When they were back outside, Nathan put his arm around Andriette's shoulder. "Maybe I should have warned you about Pearl. She is a little bawdy, but she has a sweet heart. I hope you aren't too upset that we are staying here."

"I must admit, she's a little rough." There was a nervous giggle in her voice as she answered him. "It's okay, I think."

Andriette watched as Nathan unhitched the horses and began to brush the first one down. "I'd like to help. Is there another brush?"

He looked a bit surprised and also pleased. "Sure, I'll get you one. Have you ever done this before?"

"No, but I think I can learn."

"Here you go." He stood and watched as she mimicked what she'd seen him doing. "Perfect! Thanks for the help."

Andriette smiled at him, silently jubilant at doing this job well. They worked peacefully for a few minutes, Andriette kept an eye on Nathan to see what else he did.

Dinner at the boarding house was good, and the conversation was interesting. The three miners joined Pearl, Andriette, and Nathan at the table. The men talked about copper mining. Copper prices were a concern for everyone in these mountains, if they fell too far, there would be no profit for the hard work of mining. Then the conversation turned to other concerns, such as the rivalry between the sheep men and the miners, and the constant threat of living and working in such a wild and sometimes inhospitable wilderness. Andriette enjoyed listening to the men, and began to get a sense of the politics of the area. Nathan and Andriette stood on the porch after supper, enjoying the crisp mountain air.

"Nathan," Andriette began. "This street looks a bit odd, why are so many trees cut off so high up?"

Nathan grinned and looked at her. She nearly forgot what she'd just asked as she got lost for a moment in his smile. "This town was built in 1898, in the winter time. Those trees were used to build Smizer's saloon and Sol Fuik's general store." He waited a bit, enjoying the puzzlement on her face. "It was wintertime, and the snow gets deep up here. When they were building, they cut the trees off at snow level."

"Are you saying that the snow was ten feet deep?" Andriette thought maybe he was teasing her.

"Absolutely!" He watched her face then added, "Really!"

Andriette stared down the street and tried to picture the winter snow much higher than her head. It frightened her a bit, and she wondered how she could manage. Nathan put his arm around her and held her close. "Don't worry," he whispered, "I doesn't get that deep at our cabin. We're down in the trees where it is more protected." She relaxed willing herself to put aside concerns and enjoy the moment.

Andriette didn't sleep very well that night. The room she was shown to for sleeping was a large hall with six beds lined up. She was on the third floor of the building. Everything was clean and neat, but not especially welcoming or homey. The room was big enough that it echoed with her footsteps as she chose the bed she'd use. Truthfully, Andriette was also nervous about arriving at the cabin tomorrow. She spent much of the night in prayer. At about dawn, she got up and looked out the window on the town of Battle. The town consisted of only twelve blocks. From her vantage point, she could see quite a bit of it. They'd come in on Main Street and turned on to Second. It was a rustic place with dirt streets and roughhewn log buildings and no paint, but it also beckoned her with its courageous charm and character. Down the street Andriette could see a sign for *The Battle Miner* newspaper office. Across the tops of several other buildings, she could make out the marquee over the Maine Hotel.

Breakfast was substantial; bacon and ham, eggs and pancakes. Pearl put Lillian's jelly on the table, and Andriette enjoyed it on her pancakes. Everything was delicious. The miners had little to say this morning, and looked a little haggard. Andriette suspected that they may have found the saloon after dinner last night. They did talk to Nathan about the work at the mine and were pleased to report that the price of copper was at eleven cents a pound. One gruff man with a chiseled face added, "It costs about six cents a pound to produce the copper that they ship out, so we're making a goodly profit." Nathan finished his breakfast quickly, smiled at Andriette and excused himself to go hook up the horses and prepare for the day.

Andriette, without a word, began helping Pearl clean up the table and transfer the dishes into the kitchen. Already in the kitchen when Andriette came in the first time carrying a stack of plates, Pearl looked surprised when she saw Andriette. "Lord, Girl, I can't remember the last time someone helped me clear the table."

"You don't mind, do you?"

"Of course not!" she laughed. "I don't see many women here. Mostly I have men at the boarding house."

"Aren't there women living here in Battle?" Andriette asked.

"Yes, there are some, but they stay to themselves. They don't exactly like me, with my not wearing dresses nor being a proper lady. Sometimes I get mighty lonely."

"I hear that's a danger all over these mountains."

"It is certainly a man's world up here at the top of the Divide. The work and the living ain't easy."

"How long have you been up here, Pearl?"

"I came up here in December of 1898, four years ago. This town was just getting started. Mrs. Kinsella had already started building her hotel, and she and I talked about a need for a boarding house for the miners and the herders and the wagon drivers to stay, so she added that to her plans and I've been here ever since. It's a good life, and I know that the men who stop appreciate a good meal and a clean bed."

"I know I did!" was Andriette's heartfelt response. The two women worked at washing and drying the dishes in silence until they heard footsteps in the front hall.

Nathan arrived then, and walked first to Pearl. "Thank you for the hospitality, Ma'am," he started, "We probably won't see you again for a couple of months, but you know where we are."

He held out his hand to Andriette, "Are you ready to go home?"

She took his hand and answered without hesitation, at least on the outside.

"You two take care of each other," were Pearl's parting words to them as they turned to leave.

Since Battle town site sits at the top of a mountain that also is the Continental Divide, the start of the day's trip was a steep down slope. Before they started down the grade, Nathan stopped to enjoy the view. Andriette had heard the phrase 'sweeping vista' before, and what was in front of her matched that and more.

"It would be impossible to count all the different shades of blue across this view!" she sighed quietly. They sat hand in hand and gazed at the clear sky above and in front of them. The tree covered mountains swept out below them for miles, changing hues from the deep green of the pines punctuated with bright green aspen stands, and eventually fading into a dark, velvety blue on the horizon. The mountains themselves climbed high on each side of the winding valley below, jutting ridges haphazardly across the valley floor so that it wasn't a valley at all, but more a wrinkled maze. It was the very definition of rugged and magnificent.

He let them both drink in the panorama for a few minutes, then Nathan began to point out a few landmarks. "Down there in the bottom of this hollow to the right is

Battle Lake. It is a great little lake, full of the best brook trout you'll ever eat."

Pointing towards the tallest peak, on their left, Nathan explained, "That is Bridger Peak. I'll take you there someday, to get there we go out of Battle following Second Street and up along that ridge. You can see for hundreds of miles from there on a clear day. The peak is named for Jim Bridger, a mountain man and scout who spent some time in this area. Bridger named Battle Mountain and the lake as well. The story is that he and a group of trappers fought with a combination of Arapaho, Sioux, and Cheyennes in a war party in 1841. The stream is called Battle Creek, then there's Battle Mountain, and of course the town. One story says that the trappers, with Bridger leading them, only kept from being killed because they were at the top of the mountain. They could see the warriors coming and shoot them before they got close enough to shoot the trappers with arrows."

Andriette loved hearing Nathan's stories. His letters were filled with them, and he had told her a few on the trip so far. It became clear when they began writing to one another that the love for history and the legacy that understanding brought was something they had in common.

Putting his arm around Andriette, he drew her close and began pointing. "The route we will take goes down here, then the road skirts the bottom of that ridge, and the next two in line with it. We'll turn off in the draw below that rocky ridge way down there, and we'll be almost home." He made sure she knew which ridges he meant, and she was touched by his patience and his excitement. He stopped finally and looked squarely at her, searching her face. "I've been so anxious to show you this."

She held his gaze for a moment before answering, "It's the most beautiful place I've ever seen."

His eyes told her that he knew she was being honest with him. He lingered a moment longer, looking at her, then he tenderly leaned in and kissed her gently on the nose. His voice was quiet and strong when he turned forward and said, "Let's go home."

Nathan hitched the reins and got the horses started. He told Andriette to hold on. "This is a steep old grade here, and we'll have to take it real slowly so that the wagon doesn't get away from us." He turned to her very seriously. "Andriette, if something should happen and the brake would fail, you need to jump off the wagon. I don't think that will happen, I've made this trip a hundred times, but I want you to know that if it did, you need to push yourself off to the side as best you can and get as clear of the wagon as possible. Understand?"

His seriousness was a bit alarming, though she understood why he was telling her this. "Yes, of course. Would you jump, too?"

"Yes, once I knew I couldn't get the rig back under control."

With that, they started down the mountain. Nathan held the team back and kept his foot on the brake pedal.

After they were down safely and climbing up the next grade, he relaxed. "Andri, I am sorry if I scared you."

His voice was soft and serious, and she could tell there was more.

"This is very unforgiving country. I've seen and heard about men who made one bad choice and died because of it. I love it up here, but I respect it. I understand that nature is in charge up here, and I need you to understand it, too. I want us to be happy, I want you to be happy up here like I am. We always need to think ahead and consider the possibilities."

"I think what you are saying, Nathan, is that the rules here aren't ours to make."

He turned so that he could face her. What she saw on his face was a mixture of admiration and growing respect. "That's an accurate way to put it."

The trip wasn't easy, but very enjoyable. The trees were tight and close in some spots and then opened onto lush meadows. The forest floor was thick and rich with ferns and flowers. As the sun rose above them and warmed the air, the scent of the pines was strong and fresh. Even over the sounds of the horses' hooves on the dry dirt, they could hear a choir of birds and chittering squirrels. Small streams bubbled through rocks and made delightful music for them.

Around mid-day, Nathan stopped so that they could have some lunch and rest. While he changed horses and allowed them to munch grass for a few minutes, Andriette opened a basket that Pearl generously provided for them. The breakfast at Pearl's was huge, and she thought she wasn't hungry, but the thick slices of bread and ham looked so good she couldn't resist. They sat on the grass under a tall pine and enjoyed their lunch. The sun was hot, and she could have taken a nap in this peaceful spot, but instead they gathered up the remains of the lunch and climbed back on the wagon.

About an hour later, they slogged through a fair sized creek and immediately came to a crossroad. Nathan pulled up the horses. "If we turned to the left and went downhill for about half a mile, we'd be in Copperton. It is a small way station. The dozen or so people who live there call it a town, but it isn't much. It would be the nearest place for you to go for help, though, if something ever happened to me or you needed something if I were gone. You could trust Jake Palmer, who runs the livery there. Be wary of others there, though, there are some scoundrels that seem to spend time in Copperton. In fact, California Red, a local sheep man who stays a lot in Copperton shot and killed another sheep man near there just last month."

She nodded so he would know she was paying close attention and he went on. "If we kept on this road, we'd end up in Baggs. It is on the plains and out of the mountains. It's a little smaller than Encampment, and maybe a bit closer, but the prices in the grocery there are much higher than in Encampment, so I rarely go there. Now if we turn right, we're nearly home. Which way, Ma'am?" He finished with a smile and a tip of the hat.

"Well, let's see," she teased him. "I sometimes enjoy the company of scoundrels, so we could go to Copperton, and I have money to burn, so we could go shopping in Baggs. Hmmm, I do believe I could enjoy some peace and quiet though, so how about we go right?"

"As you wish," he grinned and headed the team to the right.

They traveled about a mile and then encountered a fork in the road. The main road continued into the trees towards the left and a smaller two-tracked path sliced off to the right. Nathan turned the team right. They crossed the creek again. "This creek is the Haggarty. In the late 1830s trappers started coming into this area. In 1876, Frank Williams first staked a claim and started mining near Battle. In '96, Ben Culleton found gold at Purgatory Gulch. Then two years later, Ed Haggarty found copper up at the top of this gulch and got the Rudefeha Mine started. The creek is named for Haggarty. The town at the top, where the mine is, is called Rudefeha."

"That's a funny name," Andriette observed.

"They made it up. The letters are the first two letters of the four men who found and started the mine, Rumsey, Deal, Ferris, and Haggarty."

"That's clever, then."

"Someone did that to name a mine in Colorado."

While they were talking, they crossed the creek and started up the road, which ran parallel to the creek, going upstream. The trees were thick and tall, the air cool and damp and pungent. To the right and a little uphill, they passed a strange piece of equipment she couldn't identify, but just as she was going to ask about it, the trees began to thin, the sun shone brightly, and Andriette could see a clearing with a cabin in the middle.

Nathan pulled the horses up near the front of the cabin. They sat in the quiet for a few moments. The only sounds were the natural huffing and snorting of the horses, the creek noise far in the back ground and the chirping of a squirrel somewhere in the trees. Andriette tried to memorize every detail of her first view of her new home. The cabin was larger than she had imagined, with real glass in the windows. There was a barn for the horses back behind the house, and a small building off to the left, which she assumed was the privy. The whole area was neat and clean. The clearing was large enough that the sun was bright and cheery, with large pines ringing it to provide shelter and a feeling of protection. She took a deep breath then, and breathed in the smell of warm pine and damp earth.

"Welcome home, Mrs. Jameson." Nathan watched her reaction. He was encouraged by the look on her face and the smile in her eyes. He climbed down from the wagon and extended his hand to help her down.

She looked up at him and answered, "Thank you, Mr. Jameson. This is truly beautiful."

He hugged her then, and held her. They both stood together, enjoying the moment and becoming accustomed to the closeness. When he relaxed his hold and stepped back far enough to look at her, there were tears on her cheeks. He was at first concerned, but her self-depreciating smile put him at ease. "Can I see the inside of the cabin first?"

"Of course." He led the way.

He opened the door and stepped aside so that she could enter ahead of him. There was one large room with a dirt floor. Along the back wall on the left was a large black cook stove with ornate silver trim. Andriette knew that she would be using this both for heating and cooking. A set of shelves was built along the left wall near the stove, holding the cook pots and utensils as well as tins of food. In the opposite corner of the back wall was a four poster bed, with a thick quilt on top.

In the front half of the cabin to the left was a round pedestal table and four chairs. The table was covered by a lace tablecloth with a glass lamp in the center. There was an envelope leaned up against the lamp. To the right of the door was a hutch with drawers on the bottom and shelves on the top. Andriette's first thought was how blessed she was to be coming home to this place. She stopped in the doorway at first, but now moved into the room to take a closer look. She was in the middle of the room when she heard Nathan say, "What..?" She turned to find him smiling but surprised.

"What is it, Nathan?"

"Someone has been here while I was gone."

"What do you mean?"

"Andriette, I wanted the cabin to look good for you when we arrived, but I have never owned a lace tablecloth or a pieced quilt in my life."

It was then that he noticed the envelope on the table. He walked over and picked it up. "It is addressed to Mr. and Mrs. Nathan Jameson," he said and began to open it. Andriette peered over his shoulder.

"*We hope you don't mind that we came uninvited. Mark brought us up the day after you left for Rawlins, Nathan. We wanted your homecoming as a married couple to be special for both of you. We made the wedding ring quilt last winter, while you two were making your plans. The tablecloth was Grandma's handiwork, and the dishes we stored in the hutch were hers as well. Don't forget to water the tomato plants and the potatoes we planted in the little patch out behind the cabin. Surprise! God bless you both and remember that you will always be in our prayers and hearts. Love, Mom and Abby and Mark*"

They were both speechless. Nathan re-read the note, obviously touched. Andriette moved to the hutch and looked at the china dishes. They were lovely with small pink and yellow flowers along the edge. The set was complete with large and small plates, cups and saucers and several serving bowls. There was a polished wooden box on the hutch, and when Andriette peaked inside she discovered it held a set of silverware. Nathan finished reading and joined Andriette at the hutch. He wasn't as impressed with the china as she was, but understood what the gifts meant to her.

"Nathan, I don't know how to react to such sweetness and generosity. No one in my family would have ever thought to do such a thing as this! My father's wedding present to us was to allow his hired hand to take me to the train station. His parting words to me were, "Good luck on this crazy scheme of yours, you'll need it."

"I wouldn't know how to react to coldness like that, Andri, and I am sorry for you," he began. "But they outdid themselves this time, the little schemers." They stood together for a few more moments, absorbing the kindness and love of the gift.

"Can I show you the rest of the place?" he asked.

The pride Nathan felt in what he built was clear as he gave Andriette a tour of the homestead. Between the cabin and the barn was a nice, protected space, almost a courtyard. In one corner, where the sun would shine most of the day was a square of newly tilled ground. Three tomato seedlings were planted along one side and along the other was a mound for the potatoes. Andriette had never gardened before, but was instantly protective of this garden, started in love. As they walked around, Nathan described for her what he wanted to do in the future to make the place even better. "I'd like to make the barn larger, and of course increase the size of the cabin. Someday we might even build a new cabin, one with a wooden plank floor and two bedrooms.

Finally, they walked back down the road towards the equipment she saw on the way in. To Andriette it almost looked like the front of a steam locomotive, minus the wheels and cab. She was only a bit taller than the rounded iron sides, and two pipes that looked like smoke stacks ended high above her head. There were several doors along its side, and it took about eight of her steps to travel from one end of it to the other. Nathan began to explain it to her.

"This is a boiler. This big tank is filled with water, and I make a fire in this fire box here to heat it. The steam that is generated is converted into power here, and that power runs the saw. I have a contract with a logging outfit in the area. They cut down trees and haul them in to me. I buy the logs from them. I then cut the logs into planks and haul them up to Dillon and Rudefeha for the building and mining operations. I have a contract with the mine to supply timbers for the operation.

"Where do you get the water for the boiler? Surely you don't carry buckets from the creek!" Andriette worried.

"No, that would be a tremendous job. There's a spring right up there," he pointed up the hill. "See this hose? The other end is jammed down where the water comes out of the ground. I have a valve on this end so all I have to do is put the hose in the top of the boiler and open the valve." He turned the knob and water began flowing. "See? Running water!"

"This boiler is huge. How did you get it up here?"

"I ordered it from St. Louis, and it arrived by train in Wolcott. It was too heavy for my buckboard, of course, so I hired a freight company to haul it. It was quite a sight watching the driver steer his 20 mule team across the creek and up into here."

"Are those the logs you will cut up in to lumber?" she asked.

"Yes, but that pile won't last for very long. The boys should be bringing in a new load of logs for me in the next day or so. I'll need to get the fire stoked up and burning tonight so that the boiler is hot enough to produce power for me by tomorrow."

"Taking a week off to come get me put you behind?"

"Well," he hesitated. "It did a bit but I worked like crazy for a couple of weeks before I left to get ahead. It was worth it." He turned to her and smiled.

They stood together for a minute longer, but the horses were stamping and obviously not happy to be ignored after their hard trek through the mountains. Nathan pulled himself out of Andriette's eyes and turned to attend to the wagon. "I normally keep the wagon in the barn, but there is so much to unload, I think I'll leave it for a day or so until we've unpacked. I am sure that you will want to arrange and re-arrange how I have things stored in the kitchen and the rest of the cabin while you find places for your things. I don't want you to feel rushed."

"Thank you, that is very kind of you."

"Andriette, this is OUR home." He took her face in his hands and quietly added, "I want you to make yourself comfortable and do whatever you want inside and out. I am a bit handy as a carpenter, and I have some nice boards put aside to make shelves or anything you find you'll need. Just let me know what you want."

She had never encountered a man so willing to please, and it touched her deeply. "Nathan, if you will unload that one box with the smoked turkey and other leftovers your mother packed for us, I will see about getting us a cold dinner set out while you take care of the horses."

"That's a terrific idea," he answered her on his way to the end of the wagon for the box.

The next few days passed and settled into a happy routine for the two of them. Nathan awoke early and tended to the horses, then went out to stoke up the boiler's firebox to prepare for work. By the time he came back to the cabin, Andriette had breakfast ready for him. It took her a while to master the iron cook stove in the cabin, and Nathan was gracious and retained a sense of humor when a few of her meals turned out less than stellar. After breakfast, Nathan headed off to the saw mill for work.

"I've been here a whole week today," thought Andriette as she dried her hands and folded the dishtowel she'd been using. She pulled a chair out and sat down. She loved looking at the little hutch and the tidy cabin. It was more than she'd ever hoped for, to be the mistress of such a lovely little place. Andriette enjoyed getting moved into the cabin. She didn't change much. She'd rearranged one shelf to make room for the embroidered towels she'd brought with her. Everything seems to fit. As she sat and enjoyed the moment she remembered the satchel. She'd pushed it under the bed the evening they'd arrived and hadn't thought of it again. In a moment she was sitting at the table with the satchel at her feet. She carefully took out her white dress with the green sash. She looked forward to wearing it again when she remembered the approval in Nathan's look when she'd come down to dinner at Lillian's house. She refolded the dress carefully and placed it in the bottom drawer of a dresser against the back wall.

She reached once more into the satchel and retrieved her letters. She smiled as she remembered how she'd looked forward to receiving a letter from Nathan while she still lived in Council Bluffs. Just a glimpse of the dark strokes of his writing could lighten her day. Cradled in her lap was every note and letter he'd ever sent. She gently traced her own name on the top envelope as she considered that documented in this stack of envelopes was his shy introduction followed by their growing friendship, their sweet courtship, and finally his proposal and their wedding planning. She looked around the cabin. She needed a safe place to store these.

As she was scanning the room, Nathan's footsteps neared the cabin. He came in looking cross and tired.

"Nathan, what's wrong?"

He shrugged and answered, "I'm fine. I just nicked a tooth off the saw blade."

"Is that bad?" Andriette asked. "I mean I can tell it isn't good, but I don't understand what that means exactly."

Her eagerness to support him and learn about the mill soothed his bad mood a little. "Saw blades are darned expensive, and this one was almost new."

"Oh dear, I'm sorry. What happened?"

"There must have been a rock or a nail stuck in the pine tree I was ripping down."

"Can you run the mill with a nicked tooth on the blade?"

"No, but I have another one. It will take me an hour or so to change blades and get back to work. I was trying to hurry and wasn't as careful as I should have been. Now it's costing me time, plus I'll have to order a new blade."

Andriette put the letters on the table and got up. She took a cup off the shelf and lifted the coffee pot from the stove, praying there was still enough for a cup full. When she turned around with the steaming cup, Nathan was looking at the envelopes. "I have every one you ever sent me," she said shyly. "I have read them all so many times. I was looking for a safe place to store them."

Without a word, Nathan got up from the table and walked to a small dresser beside the bed. Andriette knew that he kept his socks and work shirts folded in the top drawer and his good shirt and pants in the bottom one. She'd not looked in those drawers, knowing they held his personal things.

He knelt down and opened the bottom drawer, rifled through the clothes, and soon stood up with a wooden box in his hands. He returned to the table, saw the coffee and smiled. "Thanks, I needed this," he said, then slid the box toward her as he motioned for her to sit down.

Andriette stared, "What a beautiful box! Did you carve the mountain scene on the top?"

"No, my talent with wood stops at two by fours and an occasional shelf. My grandfather made this box and carved the top. He was a true craftsman."

"He certainly was," replied Andriette. "This is very intricate work."

Nathan sipped his coffee. The creases in his forehead smoothed, his earlier cross attitude forgotten. "Maybe there's enough room in there for those letters."

Andriette lifted the tiny brass latch and opened the lid. She smiled when she recognized the top envelope in the box. Her own handwriting greeted her.

"I've read every one of those so many times I have some of them memorized," he admitted. "I reckon your collection of letters belongs with my own collection."

Andriette was speechless. She was touched to her soul that he treasured her letters as much as she treasured his. They sat in silence while Nathan finished his coffee. Finally, he put the cup down and stood up. Andriette stood up and found herself wrapped in his arms. They enjoyed the moment a while longer, then drew apart. "I really have to go back to work," he said. "I just came up to get some tools out of the barn."

When he'd shut the door, Andriette admired the beautiful box again, then decided that it belonged on the china hutch where she could see it and enjoy it.

***

In the weeks that followed, Andriette worked to make the small cabin feel homey and efficient for their needs. She used some of the cloth she had brought with her to make curtains for the three windows in the cabin. She tended to the garden. Once or twice a week, she baked bread, and every day after she cleaned up breakfast, she planned what she would cook for that night's supper. The creek was about a thirty yards to the north of the cabin, and every morning she carried water enough for the whole day so that Nathan wouldn't have to.

After several hours in the small cabin each day when she finished her work, Andriette began wandering down to the sawmill. At first she just watched, but soon she realized that there were small ways that she could help there, to make Nathan's work go quicker. She noticed that as he ran a log through the saw, there were odds and ends pieces of wood that fell from the saw that were not big enough or were the wrong size for him to sell. These were the pieces that Nathan used to keep the boiler hot. She began picking these pieces up and stacking them near the fire pot of the boiler. Soon, she began stoking the fire pot to keep it hot.

For the first few days, Nathan said nothing, but smiled at her as he passed her while he worked. As the weeks went by, though, he began to coach her on how to stoke the firebox more efficiently and ask her to do other small jobs for him. He was always careful to thank her and let her know he appreciated her help.

Andriette, even with working beside Nathan for several hours a day, took time to go off by herself. She enjoyed wonderful walks through the woods. Behind the barn and up the hill a short distance was a small meadow that she adored. It was a small natural clearing filled with tall grass and wild flowers of all kinds. At one edge of the meadow was a huge rock. It seemed out of place because there were no other rocks nearby even close to its size. The rock stood up about three feet high with a smooth side which faced east into the meadow. It was the perfect place to sit, with her back against the rock, warm and inviting, to read and study her Bible and to pray.

Chapter 8

August 18, 2007 afternoon

Hannah locked the gate behind her and returned to her car. During the week there wasn't usually a lot of traffic on the highway, but this was a common route between Encampment and Baggs, so she paid no attention when she heard a vehicle on the highway behind her. She didn't notice that the green pickup slowed a bit while the driver on the highway behind her took in the scene.

A long standing tradition for Hannah and her dad was to take a walk around the property after they were settled in. Hannah unloaded her supplies and put them away. She struggled with the full cooler, but got it situated under a counter in the kitchen. Then, she filled a water bottle and added it to a small rucksack she liked to hike with. The bag held granola bars and a few survival essentials. Her dad insisted that she carried it with her any time she left the cabin, and he'd carried one as well. "Don't get too comfortable in the woods, Hannah," he'd say. "You can't ever know what you'll find, and the time to decide you need something isn't when you are lost in the woods."

Hannah checked the sky and smiled. The trees were so tall and straight that there was only a view of the sky looking nearly overhead, but what she saw was pure blue above her. She stood for a moment, absorbing the vibrance of the day. Everything here always seemed to be in high definition. The blue of the sky contrasted with the greens in the trees and the grass, punctuated by the amazing variety of flowers creating a carpet before her.

The property she now owned was only ten acres, not really very large in the grand scheme, but large enough to feel as if she were alone in the world as she walked. While it was basically a square shape, it was set on point to the highway close by with the gate and driveway creating the south-pointing bottom point. Walking slowly, she allowed herself to fully enjoy the land and the day. The terrain was steep in many places, and at this altitude Hannah sometimes stopped to catch her breath while looking for the landmarks she always enjoyed seeing. She scrambled to the top of the huge outcropping of granite rocks which marked the east corner of her land and sat down, out of breath but euphoric at the view into the eastern valley below. She and her father sat here many times, sometimes to watch elk grazing in the small meadow. One summer they watched a small herd of mamas and their newborn calves. The calves were old enough in that late summer to be kicking up their heels. She was delighted with their games of tag. Smiling at the memory, Hannah's eyes suddenly filled with tears. Her father's common sense and wisdom about life were precious to her. She gained much by her time here with her dad, and the knowledge that she'd never sit with him again on this rock hit her like a splash of cold water.

Shaking off the sadness, she continued on her survey. Now she was heading north and a little west. The terrain was steep for a while, then it opened up to a high grassy arena, not a meadow, and not yet above timberline, but with only a few trees around the edges. The grass was about as tall as her knees and shared the ground with a bounty of wild flowers in every hue of yellow and purple. High mountain wild flowers have a short lifespan, but use their time to the fullest with the variety of color and shape they display. There were tiny white stars, azure bells on tall straight stalks, and flowers with a light purple fringe of petals surrounding large bright yellow centers. Her favorites were the Queen Anne's lace growing taller than her head at the edge of the trees and the tiny wild strawberry plants hugging the ground in the open.

Hannah stopped and closed her eyes to listen. The clearing was alive with the sounds of buzzing bees and other insects. The quick, harsh brrrrp of grasshoppers as they flew punctuated the music like a snare drum. The sun was warm on her back as she stood there, and she felt at peace.

Hannah opened her eyes as a new, larger sound entered her awareness. Ahead of her at the edge of the clearing were two elk, feeding lazily in the quiet shadows. Hannah remained still as she watched them amble along, munching the grass they tore from the earth. *Thank you,* she whispered a silent prayer. She was still on the outs with God, but couldn't help feeling that seeing these amazing creatures at ease in their home was a special gift from above. Though she hadn't moved, something alerted the elk to her presence. They lifted their heads and looked squarely at her and froze. She stared back at them, trying to silently send them a message of good will and that she brought them no harm. After a few seconds, they were satisfied that she wasn't a threat, and moved calmly off into the trees and out of sight.

At the top corner of the property was a gnarled old pine tree she called the Top Tree. Hannah sat down with her back to the tree and pulled out an apple and her water. She rested there for a few minutes, absently eating the snack and letting her mind wander. Her job as a graphic design artist for a large advertising firm was the career she had always wanted. She worked hard through college to become the best she could be, and she had a natural talent for seeing how an ad campaign could best be created.

She'd been so excited at the end of her senior year when the firm sent her a letter asking her to come to Denver for an interview. She jumped at the chance and loved the operation from the beginning. Two days after graduation, she packed her things into her car and moved sixty miles south to a small apartment in Aurora, within biking distance of her new office.

It didn't bother her that she wasn't on the actual Design and Marketing team. Those guys had the stress of creating new ideas and pitching them to the client. The pressure to always be new and innovative was something Hannah didn't enjoy. Instead, she worked with several D & M teams after their ideas were created and accepted. She got to sit at her computer table and actually create what the team thought up. She got a lot of satisfaction in watching someone's idea become reality on her screen. It was a challenge and used her creativity. Sometimes she made a suggestion that improved the original idea, and those were the times she loved the best.

That's where her problem at work started. William Bates was the senior ad agent for one of the D & M teams she worked with. He was young and competitive. A month ago, she was assigned to work on one of his ideas for a small but upcoming architectural firm. She made some changes to the wording and layout of original idea of the marketing brochure they were creating, to make it clearer and better. She added her changes to the draft, finished it up and sent it on. Mitch Radford, one of the company's three VPs, happened to see the brochure before William did, and recognized the changes that Hannah made. In the staff meeting that Friday, in front of all the D & M teams as well as all the artists, Mitch singled her out and complimented her for seeing the problem with the original idea and taking the initiative to correct and improve the brochure. Hannah's pride at having a good job recognized was very short lived when a raging William Bates came into her office a few minutes after the staff meeting ended.

"If you ever do that again, you conniving little tart, I will make sure you are looking for a new job before the end of the week."

His face was red with anger. He spoke very quietly, though, and no one else could hear their conversation. "I will not have some glorified secretary changing my ideas and then cuddling up to Mitch for a pat on the back. Watch yourself."

Just like that he was gone, but the anger and ugliness of the encounter left Hannah shaking. She certainly hadn't meant to make him look bad, and she hadn't ever even talked to Mitch Radford except in staff meetings, let alone 'cuddled up' with him. She hated the innuendo that she conducted herself inappropriately with a boss, and she was frightened at having made an enemy in the company, especially one who was as powerful and influential as William. In the three weeks since that ugly interchange, William said several things to Hannah in front of others that put down her work. He was overly critical of everything she'd done and embarrassed her twice with pointing out errors in rough drafts she was still working on as if they were final copy. Hannah was worried about how his slams would affect the other designers' view of her.

As she sat in the woods, Hannah considered the situation. She wished for the hundredth time that her dad was still around to listen and advise her on what to do. She loved her job, and thus far had just ducked her head and said nothing to William's attacks, but she didn't foresee them stopping until he fully defeated her. She didn't know if her present course of action was the best one, or if she should stand up to him or talk to someone else in the company. Dad would have known what she should do, and thinking about it made her angry at him all over again for choosing not to pursue more chemo therapy after the first two rounds were unsuccessful.

Sighing, Hannah tossed her apple core under a tree and put her water back into her rucksack. There was nothing to gain with obsessing over her work trouble, she'd already been doing that to no avail. She took a deep breath and squared her shoulders. Putting everything out of her mind was the goal, and that would be easy for the rest of her walk. Her favorite part of the property was this west side.

With the Top Tree behind her, Hannah was soon into thick trees. The way was mostly downhill here on this side, and even though there wasn't a path, Hannah knew the way without hesitation. She wound her way through the forest, stepping over fallen trees and the thick undergrowth of ferns and grasses. Here and there she'd have to walk around marshy spots created by natural springs. Water bubbled out of the ground in several spots on the upper west side of her mining claim, and the wonder of it made her smile. Down a bit farther, the trickling water of several brooks conjoined to create a small stream that eventually ran into the Haggarty at the bottom of the Gulch.

Hannah worked her way down the mountainside. She didn't go all the way to the western corner of the mining claim, and instead skirted around a rocky point and dropped back toward the south. Under the rocks of that point, Hannah knew, was a small cave, about six feet high at its tallest and only about twelve feet into the side of a rocky hillside. She and her father enjoyed many conversations about the cave, trying to figure out if it was a natural occurrence, or if it was the beginning of some old prospector's mine shaft that had caved in except at the opening. Hannah explored it with her father, and they were brave enough to shine their flashlights into it when Dad felt sure it was uninhabited. Normally, they steered clear, though, because the mountain lion lived somewhere in this area.

The trees grew more dense here. The going was tougher, with more deadfall to climb over or around. Hannah always looked forward to this part of the 'survey walk' because this area held a special surprise. She could now hear Haggarty Creek below her about two hundred yards downhill and to the west. She angled uphill a bit and soon saw what she was looking for. The old cabin dated back to the time that Dillon was in full swing. It was a small place hidden in the trees, with a spring nearby. She stepped over a fallen tree trunk and then sat down on it. Taking a deep breath, she closed her eyes and listened to the silence of the forest, not at all silent in reality. A squirrel chirped from the top of a tree, there were all kinds of buzzes around her, and the wind made the tops of the pines rustle gently. She opened her eyes to take in the scene. The cabin was small, only one room, and the walls were only three or four logs high now. The forest was slowly reclaiming its land from the efforts of someone now long gone. Hannah sat remembering what the cabin looked like when she'd first seen it. Most of the walls had been intact then, and a part of the roof was still on.

The place was strewn with broken china and pottery. Two wonderfully old bottles had been in the corner of the cabin on a shelf. Hannah could picture them as she'd first seen them, while now they adorned a shelf in her own cabin not far away.

It seemed, with the broken dishes all around, that maybe something sad happened here, yet this site always filled Hannah with peace. She tried imagining what life would have been like for someone living here, so isolated yet also so protected and snug inside these trees and mountains.

She breathed in deeply, trying to absorb the peace of the quiet morning in this place. There was certainly a hollow spot inside her heart created by her father's absence, but even that seemed a little smaller here as she enjoyed the moment.

Finally, feeling rested and refreshed, Hannah stood up and headed south and east, down toward the sound of the Haggarty. She found a huge fallen log over the creek bed, and tight roped across the creek to the other side. She walked only a few yards beyond the creek and easily found the two track road that would lead her safely back to her cabin. Along the road, the trees were a little thinner, and the sun was warm on her face.

As she approached the end of her walk, she looked down in the dust of the road, and a memory greeted her there. On the first day of their trip to the cabin when Hannah was fourteen, they made their traditional 'survey trip' around the claim. The weather that year was dry, and as they returned to the cabin, retracing the final hundred or so yards over their route out along the road, Dad stopped suddenly and peered down at the footprints. He backtracked twice and stared. Hannah was hot and a little tired, she watched a bird flitting in the trees for a few moments and then became impatient with his actions until he called her to him. "Hannah, look at the tracks in the road." He said it softly.

She focused on the road then, and saw her outbound footprints along the dusty trail next to her father's larger ones. She noticed that his stride was still longer than hers, but not as much longer as they used to be. "Does the fact that I take more steps than you mean that I walk twice as far?" She loved to tease him about his long legs.

"Look closer, Hannah, you are missing something."

His voice was quiet with a more excited tone than he'd had all morning. She looked again, studying the path of their footprints and looking carefully. Her father stood patiently, waiting for her to make the discovery herself. When she finally saw it, her eyes grew wide. "Dad, why are the cat tracks over the top of my tracks?"

They squatted down to study the dirt. Hannah's shoe prints were clear. Inside many of her prints, as well as around them, were the clear tracks of an animal. Hannah knew that what she was seeing was a mountain lion's prints and that the animal traveled in the same direction as they had. "Well, Hannah, it looks like this cat wanted to see what we were up to. She must have either seen us or smelled us, and decided to check us out. Look how her prints are cleaner than your prints underneath. That's how we can know that we walked here first, and then she came after. If we walked over her prints, then her tracks would have been smudged, but your prints are smudged."

"How do you know it is her, and not a male?"

"Well, I don't, really. We've not seen any signs of babies for the last couple of summers, so maybe the old female isn't around anymore. This print is smaller than ones we've seen before, so I'm guessing that this is a young female. I don't think she's fully grown, maybe a couple of years."

Hannah wasn't hot or tired any longer. They followed their own prints back up the road seeing that the cat's tracks were right over them. Where their prints moved off into the trees, they lost the trail. "How long do you think she followed us, Dad?"

"I have no idea, maybe a long way, maybe just this far."

"How close do you think she got to us?" Hannah was nervous at the thought of the mountain lion stalking them.

"There's no way to tell, really. I'm guessing she was relatively close by."

"Dad, that's scary."

He looked her in the eyes. "If she wanted to attack us, she'd have done it. A mountain lion is a powerful creature, and she has the advantage. But Girl, there is a lot of game in these mountains, and that lion has plenty to eat. What she doesn't have is a lot of excitement. Now, look at today from her point of view. She is out for a stroll and she comes across a new scent. Maybe she heard us and that first got her attention. She just wanted to see what was happening in her land. Either way, we didn't seem to pose any threat to her so after she checked us out for a little while, she went her own way. It isn't something to be frightened about."

"Are you sure she wasn't just saving us for dinner?"

Dad laughed then, and hugged her close. "Hannah, I don't think we'd taste very good, certainly not as good as a deer. At any rate," he paused and his voice got soft again, "Today we connected with a marvelous beast, and that, Hannah, is a gift not many people get."

He held her shoulders and looked seriously at her. "That lion knows you now. She's connected to you. She will always recognize your scent, next summer and for years to come."

"How long can a mountain lion live, Dad?" Hannah asked.

"In the wild, they can live about 10 years."

Hannah thought about that day so many years ago. She wondered if the same mountain lion still lived on this mountain. Smiling at the thought, she opened the back door of the cabin and went inside to rest.

Chapter 9

July 15, 1902

From the first night they arrived at the cabin, Nathan slept out in the barn. He made it clear to Andriette that he wanted her, but only when she was ready. She never was wholly comfortable with Nathan sleeping outside of his own cabin, but he insisted.

One evening, after supper was finished and Andriette's kitchen was cleaned up, she went outside to see what Nathan was doing. She found him at the barn, fixing a strap on one of the horse's halters. They chatted while he finished up, then decided to take a walk together as the evening came to a close.

They ended up in the upper meadow, and Andriette pointed out the rock she found. "It is such a peaceful spot to pray and think," she told him. They sat together, shoulders touching with their backs against the rock, watching the clouds overhead change from white to pink to orange and finally to a deepening purple as the sun set behind them. Nathan reached over and took her hand, holding it gently in his. They sat in silence, enjoying. Just as twilight began in earnest, Andriette was startled by the sound of a woman screaming. It came from the northwest, probably beyond the creek. It sounded to Andriette as if the woman was in horrible pain or terrible fear. She jumped up and looked at Nathan.

"Nathan, we need to go help her!" She didn't understand why he wasn't as alarmed as she about this incongruous sound.

He stood slowly and took her hand back in his. His voice was serious, but his eyes were smiling at her. "Andri, that isn't a woman in trouble, even though it sounds just like it could be. That is a mountain lion, and I am sure she doesn't need our help."

"A mountain lion?" Andriette couldn't quite understand how what she heard wasn't what she'd thought.

"She is probably hunting. I've seen her a few times. Mostly I've seen her watching me. She has a den up over on that hillside." He motioned to the north and west. "You'd do well not to walk off into the trees in that direction, especially in the spring when her cubs are little, but probably she has already spotted you on your walks and decided you aren't much of a threat to her."

The idea of a mountain lion watching her as she walked alone in the trees was a bit unnerving, and her thoughts must have shown on her face. Nathan pulled her to him and held her tight. "Don't worry. There are lots of things in these woods that she would rather eat than you. There is plenty of game here for her. She can hear and smell so much better than we can, that she'll see you long before you are too close to her."

"What does she eat, small animals?"

He chuckled. "She'll take down a full sized deer about once a week. More than that when she's feeding cubs."

"Oh dear. Lions are really powerful. I had no idea." Andriette was quiet for a moment and then looked up at her husband. "I have fallen in love with these woods, and I have felt really safe here. It never occurred to me that there could be dangerous animals here, though now that I think about it, of course there are."

"The only two real threats are the lions and the bears. The lions I don't worry about at all. They actually are very timid creatures in relation to man. That old girl you heard is the queen of this area. Mountain lions are territorial, they establish their territory and others respect it. She'll get a visit every couple of years from a male, but he won't stay long, and then she'll have cubs to raise the next spring. When they get big enough, they'll move off and find their own territory."

"What about the bears?"

"Bears can be nasty, and they are easier to startle. We have brown bears, which aren't always brown in color, and grizzlies. I haven't ever seen signs of grizzlies around the cabin, but once in a while there are browns. You usually can smell them before you can see them.

"I make enough noise around here every day with the sawmill that bears won't be nearby. Now, when you go out walking if you smell something horrible or see a bear, just be noisy and go in the other direction. They say you should never look at a bear in the eye, that challenges them."

It was getting dark, so they began to walk, hand in hand, back to the cabin. Even knowing there were bears and lions in the woods didn't scare her with Nathan beside her. When they were back at the cabin, Andriette stopped and faced Nathan. She studied his face and then her own heart. She realized that she cared for him because of his letters, even before she ever saw his face. She knew that she respected and trusted him as well. She knew they were a good partnership and she enjoyed working with him at the mill and being with him. It became clear, then, not as a bolt of lightning but as a reassurance deep within her, that she loved him.

He watched her in the moments they stood in the cool evening and guessed, by the look in her eyes, that a decision was made. It was the same decision that he had made the day she first came to help him at the sawmill.

"I love you, Andriette." He said it simply and quietly.

"And I love you, Nathan."

She took his hand and led him into their home. Neither of them was disappointed.

Chapter 10

August 19, 2007

As the sun streamed into the window above her head, Hannah stretched and smiled. When she'd returned from her survey walk yesterday, she'd made a great lunch and ate it on the deck. She'd tidied up the cabin and then spent the day reading in the hammock out back. Towards evening, she'd taken a little walk down to the creek and back.

She'd slept well and felt good as she got up. After drinking her tea and eating granola and yogurt, she decided that she was up for a hike. She added some food and water to her rucksack, grabbed her camera and set off. It was three miles from the highway to Dillon, mostly uphill.

The road up Haggarty Gulch was a public road, though few ever drove on it. Hannah walked west from her cabin, crossed over the split rail fence that marked the property boundary here, and found the jeep trail. Only four-wheel drive vehicles or ATVs could manage the rough conditions. It was a terrific road to walk, but for a vehicle it was a challenge due to the rocks and holes and because of the tight turns and low branches. She always pictured what it would have been like to drive this road in a wagon. She knew that the people then must have been more stout and intrepid than she. As she walked, Haggarty Creek ran to her right. Sometimes she could watch it cascading right beside her, sometimes she could only hear it below her. This was a deep gulch, and the sun filtered through the trees sparingly. It was warm, though, and soon Hannah's sweatshirt was tied around her waist as the road climbed gradually.

She came to the first of two creek crossings. There were no bridges here, so crossing the Haggarty meant getting your feet wet. Hannah watched the water of the creek dance over the boulders and rocks. The clarity of the water made it easy to see the bottom. In some spots the water could be waist deep or more, but here it wasn't more than five or six inches, unless your foot slipped off a rock and into a hole. Hannah decided that she didn't want to get her feet wet, so she opted to leave the road for the next mile and stay on the high side. She climbed a small ridge and then followed the top of the ridge to where the road crossed back over the creek. The ridge was only about 100 yards up, but at this altitude, it was work for Hannah, and she stopped for a drink and to catch her breath at the top. The trees were thinner here, and she soaked up the warmth of the sun as she rested. The rest of the walk to the second crossing was easier, she rejoined the road and made good time again.

At the top, the Haggarty Gulch opens onto a huge high mountain valley. The creek itself hugs the base of the mountains, falling off to the right of the road. Very soon, Hannah could no longer see or hear it. She didn't mind, though. Surrounded by high, timber filled ridges; the valley that housed the town of Dillon was a warm, sheltered surprise. Here, the trees were farther apart and the grass was as tall as Hannah's waist. Wild flowers peeked out from every lichen covered rock. Hannah stopped to gather wild raspberries on one curve of the road, eating them as she continued on. Then she picked a handful of wild strawberries, small but very sweet, at the next curve. Right before the last lazy turn in the road before Dillon came into view, Hannah stopped to drink from the spring she and her Dad found years before. While he was always careful about not drinking out of the creek, they often stopped to get a refreshing drink at this spring. The water bubbled merrily out of the rocks, tasting sweet and cold enough to shock your throat.

As she enjoyed a rest and the coolness of the water, Hannah heard a familiar sound and smiled. The sheep. This high valley provided prime grazing land for sheep since before the miners came for the copper. Basque sheepherders tended flocks up here in the summer for years. Hannah enjoyed beautiful artwork along with names and dates carved into trees as the sheepherders left tangible proof of their legacy carved into the white bark of the aspens all through this valley and many others in the Sierra Madres. Continuing on up the road, Hannah kept watch for the sheep herder's wagon. Soon she spotted the flock off to her right, closer to the creek. She stopped and watched as the sheep calmly tore at the grass while two huge white Great Pyrenees dogs kept watch. She knew that there was nothing to fear from the dogs unless she approached the sheep, then they'd put themselves between her and the sheep, attacking if necessary, not allowing her to get too close. She and Dad once had a close encounter with the dogs when the sheep were grazing right on the road. They walked up the road, toward the sheep. The dogs reacted decisively, not making a sound but signaling their distrust with their stance and their eyes. Hannah's dad stood calmly while Hannah cowered behind him until the shepherd saw them and whistled for the dogs.

Today, with the sheep far off the road, the dogs wouldn't give her a second thought. Hannah kept walking and soon spotted the sheepherder's wagon, nestled at the edge of the trees. It was a traditional sheep wagon, with its characteristic shape, like a loaf of bread. She saw that today was laundry day – the herder had three brightly colored shirts stretched over bushes near the wagon, drying in the sun. A beautiful chestnut colored mare was picketed nearby. Hannah continued to walk, and finally saw the herder step out from the other side of the wagon. His practiced eyes scanned the area. He saw her and waved. She waved back.

Hannah often speculated that the herder's life was peaceful and calm, though her dad told her that many lambs each year are taken by the lions, coyotes and bears in the area.

Add that to the loneliness and the challenge of keeping all the sheep together in this rough country in spite of wicked summer storms and early August snows, and it would be a tough life. Still, it seemed serene and romantic to her.

Hannah was nearing the end of her uphill trek. The valley widened out even more here, and the basin she entered opened into a beautiful meadow of tall grass and a few short trees. She was now on Main Street, Dillon, Wyoming. A casual visitor to this meadow may not ever know that he was walking through the center of a frontier town, because the remnants of civilization had all but disappeared due to the effects of weather and time. As she continued into the heart of town, she knew where to look to see the vague outlines of the foundations of the mercantile, the hotel and the boarding house.

Hannah stopped in the center of town and sat on a huge flat granite rock. She pulled her water bottle and a Clif Bar from her rucksack and looked around. The sky was a pure, deep blue. All around her the mountains formed a tall barrier to the outside world, and as Hannah sat there she felt safe and secure. The day was warm and the sun's warmth radiated back to Hannah from the rock. The breeze was light and gentle. Hannah took in the sky above her, not a cloud anywhere. She sighed.

She loved the fact that the serenity of this place always helped her to gain perspective on her life and make big decisions. It was on this very rock that she chose to accept a scholarship to the University of Northern Colorado in Greeley, Colorado instead of the offer she'd received from University of Nebraska. She smiled as she remembered how she agonized over the decision for several weeks before their trip, fearing she'd hurt her dad's feeling by choosing to go far away and not attending 'his' college. She remembered vividly how sitting here she realized he hadn't put any pressure on her while she made her decision because he truly wanted her to make the decision for herself. As she'd sat here that day, the choice was clear, UNC gave her more of what she needed to build herself a career and a life, and Dad and Mom would support her wholeheartedly.

The weight of the decision lifted off of her and the day became brighter instantly.

Looking back, she knew that going to UNC had indeed been a good decision for her. She discovered her passion for advertising and graphics while at the same time learning to be a person independent of her parents.

With that, a cloud entered her thoughts, returning her to the problems she faced now. The independence and freedom she embraced in college seemed to be at the foundation of her trouble with Greg. He loved her, of that she was certain, but he didn't understand her need for space or to make her own decisions. He had been raised in a very conservative Christian home and expected her to be satisfied with being a wife and stay-at-home mom when they married. He hadn't ever actually asked her to marry him, but for several months the topic was constantly with them. He'd just assumed she'd marry him, and assumed she'd quit work soon after and start a family. Hannah frowned as she remembered their last, final blow up.

They were sitting at dinner at one of his favorite small diners in Lodo, lower downtown Denver. Hannah never liked the place, the food was often greasy and the wait staff were all large chested girls with doe eyes and flirty smiles. Greg liked to tease with them and had been especially warm with their server that night. Hannah was irritated.

She'd been telling Greg about the way William Bates charged into her office that morning and threatened her. She wanted him to support her and help her work through the best way to handle the situation. Instead, he seemed distracted. Their blond waitress brought their dinners, a salad for Hannah and a huge burger with extra fries for Greg. Greg watched her retreat, then turned to Hannah.

"I had a call today from Bill in Minneapolis. A spot just opened in their corporate law division and they want me there in two weeks."

Hannah was so jarred by his abrupt change of topic, and hurt by his inattention to her that it took several seconds for his words to sink in.

"Minneapolis?" she finally squeaked out.

"Babe, this will be perfect. The position has a nice raise attached, so you won't even need to worry about finding a job. I'll go to Minneapolis and find an apartment, you can plan a small wedding, then give notice and join me."

"Greg, I like my job," was all Hannah could manage.

"Really?" Greg's voice took on an air of condescension. "What have you just spent the last half hour griping about, Hannah? This will solve your problem. You can spend your days taking care of me instead of sitting at a computer screen."

Greg continued, oblivious to all else, talking about how prominent this position was and how he'd be in line for partnership in just a few years. Then he started talking about buying a house in the next year, one with three bedrooms so it would be big enough for the family they'd have. Hannah quit listening. Sirens were blaring inside her head. She knew, in a moment of intense clarity, that what he was planning wasn't her life. It wasn't what she wanted. Somewhere deep inside, her heart was cracking, she did love Greg, and she had envisioned their lives together. Always in her dreams though, it was a meshing of their lives, not of her giving up all she'd worked for and loved in exchange for living his life.

Slowly the sirens faded and the clatter of dishes and the conversations around her returned. She knew what needed to be said, what needed to be done.

Greg was still talking. He hadn't noticed she'd gone away and was just now returning. "We'll trade in your little Chevy and get you a small SUV, so that you have plenty of room for toting babies. If we do it soon, then it will still be a new car but we will have it nearly paid off by the time we actually have children to put in the back seat." He met her eyes then, and his smile was one of pure happiness. He was snug in his vision of a perfect future, and Hannah felt pangs of sadness at what she was about to say.

"Greg, we care very much for each other, of that I am sure. You are a terrific man, and you will be a wonderful husband and father."

Greg smiled at her words, not yet grasping what was coming.

"I'm sorry, but I know for sure that I won't be the one sharing your life with you." Hannah regretted that he hadn't ever given her a ring. It would have been a good closing to slip it off her finger and lay it on the table in front of him. Instead, she stood up slowly and walked around to his side of the table. She bent down and kissed him gently on the forehead, then simply walked away.

In the next few weeks, she'd wrestled with many second thoughts. She vacillated between absolute confidence that she'd done the right thing and berating herself for being selfish and mean. She questioned again and again whether her decision, made in such a quick moment, was wise or fool hearty. Greg called her many times, and through his incredulity, then anger, then resigned regret, she found a growing strength in the knowledge that she hadn't been happy with his controlling ways. Even though she became convinced that breaking it off was the right thing, after their last conversation the crack in her heart opened up and she felt a deep hurt at his absence. She feared she would never find someone to share her life with, and she felt alone and foolish.

With work issues, the breakup and Dad's death what had been left of her heart disintegrated completely.

Hannah continued to look around Dillon from her perch. The sun was hot on her back, bees and deer flies zoomed past her. She sat, emptying her mind, hoping, maybe even praying. She wasn't even sure what for.

Hannah's thoughts once more crowded in, but these thoughts were new. They weren't recriminating and negative. She began to tune into the beauty around her and let it infuse her with hope. She was alone. Greg was her past. She allowed herself to accept that she'd made a good decision. Her dad was gone. She'd miss him every day for the rest of her life, but that was okay and not an indication of some character flaw.

"Do your best Hannah, try your hardest, and then be satisfied with who, what, and where you are." Dad's words

came so clearly into her mind, she couldn't swear that she hadn't heard them out loud.

She sat for a while longer, absorbing the warmth of the day and the internal warmth that came to her. Finally she roused herself and began the hike back to the cabin. She felt lighter. Accepting the circumstances that surrounded her wasn't going to be easy, but she could do it. *I'm strong and smart and in control of myself,* thought Hannah, *and that is exactly where I want to be.*

Chapter 11

August 15, 1902

Andriette sat with her back to her 'prayer rock'. She looked around her at the rough and wild beauty of the meadow and thought about the last two months. When she arrived, she'd been confident in herself and her decision, but still somewhat unsure of Nathan. In the eight weeks she had been with him at the cabin, her confidence in him had grown. She was satisfied with her life in all aspects and deeply in love with her husband. She sat in the warm sunshine and marveled at the way God worked out all the details to provide the blessings she could now count.

She spent every day with Nathan. She met the two men he bought logs from when they delivered a new load to him. They were quiet men, very shy of her. One day, they stayed and ate dinner at the cabin, but said very little beyond "Thank you, Ma'am."

She enjoyed the hours she spent with Nathan, whether at their cabin or taking evening walks, or helping him at the mill. She watched Nathan work and was amazed by his strength. When he worked it was like a well-choreographed dance. Each movement telegraphed purpose and seemed to lead into the next motion. No energy was wasted on unnecessary work. She marveled at some of the slings and contrivances Nathan engineered to help him move larger logs.

Though she was alone often, she was not lonely. She especially enjoyed her solitary walks in the mornings. Each walk was a blessing and an adventure. She was delighted with each different kind of wild flower she found, impressed at the creativity and variety of God's creation. She enjoyed the wildlife as well, and now knew where the old porcupine liked to sit during the day and where a few of the blue jays built their nests. She caught glimpses of a fox and her kits as well as many deer.

Now that it was August, she enjoyed finding wild raspberries and strawberries. She began taking a basket with her each morning to gather them as she found them. Nathan smiled and joined her excitement to have such a treat for dessert.

Andriette was content as she had never been before. As she sat at the rock, she began to pray. *Lord, you have given me so much that I know I can't earn and don't deserve. Thank you, God for these blessings and for this time. I hope that this life with Nathan goes on forever, Lord, but no matter what happens, I ask you to help me always to feel and be as close to you, and to Nathan as I am right now.* She sat quietly and gathered in the feeling of sitting in God's presence. *Lord, please bless Jed and Walt who bring Nathan wood. Give them strength and safety.* Andriette continued her prayer, asking for God's protection and blessing on her family and Nathan's. Then, she finished her prayer. *God, this is such a beautiful spot you've created. Thank you for the warmth of this rock and the beauty around it. Lord, I ask that you protect and bless anyone who ever sits in this spot. Give that person protection and peace and safety from all harm, as you have given to me here. Thank you Father, Amen.*

Andriette gathered up her basket of fresh raspberries and walked back to the cabin. The mill was quiet, the saw wasn't running, and Nathan had the horses hitched to the buck board. "Did you have a nice walk?" he asked as she approached.

"Yes, I did, and I found a basket full of raspberries. I wish I knew how to make jam."

"Walt and Jed just left a few minutes ago. They are on their way to Encampment with a wagon of lumber that we loaded, but they also brought me a message that Allen Murphy needs a load up at Dillon. Would you like to go with me to Dillon to deliver?"

Chapter 12

August 20, 2007

Hannah saved a visit to her cherished spot on the property for the next morning. She awoke early and grabbed an apple and her rucksack and took off. She crossed Haggarty Creek and headed to the center of the diamond. After about 15 minutes of walking, she began glancing to her left, into the heart of her land, to catch a first glimpse of a little meadow. She walked for about a hundred yards until she reached the middle. This was a place she considered nearly magical. As a child she played here for hours, singing or dancing, or staring at interesting bugs. She took afternoon naps here, using the soft grasses and flowers as a blanket beneath her and her jacket rolled as a pillow. Many times, she and Dad carried sleeping bags and snacks up here and slept the night.

"Daddy?"

"Yes, Hannah?"

"How many stars do you think there are up there?" Nine-year-old Hannah lay on her back, tucked into her sleeping bag. Nights in the mountains, even in August, often saw temperatures in the low 40s. This night was cloudless, moonless and clear, the perfect combination for star gazing. Hannah put her hand up towards the stars, they seemed close enough to touch.

"Only God knows that, Sweetie."

A falling star streaked across the sky then, and Hannah's questions were lost in awe.

As Hannah stood in the sunshine of the meadow and that night, she shook her head. They were fearless when they were together. Hannah couldn't imagine sleeping alone with a talkative child in the middle of this meadow now. While she felt perfectly safe and content in the cabin last night all alone, she had no desire to be out in these woods by herself at night.

Hannah left the middle of the meadow and walked to the western edge of it. Her goal was a large granite boulder with veins of mica mottling through it. The only rock of its size anywhere near, this rock seemed out of place in some ways, but Hannah always considered it the hub of the meadow. As she approached, she noticed the smooth stones that created a v-shape in front of the boulder. They always looked to her like an arrow pointing to it. Somehow, she pictured God placing the boulder and the smaller stones here and then creating the meadow to complement them. She touched the rough, straight side of the boulder, feeling the warmth it absorbed from the heat of the alpine sun. *There is always peace here,* Hannah thought. *It doesn't matter what stress is going on in the world or my life, this spot can't be touched by it.*

Hannah let the peacefulness and calm seep into her. She felt the last of the tension leave her neck and shoulders. Here, in this meadow near the top of the world, ordinary problems became smaller and easier to put in to perspective. She didn't let herself think about specific issues, but she knew that this was why she'd come. The ability to prioritize was so hard for her. The skill of relegating problems to their rightful place and not letting them be much bigger than they really are wasn't a skill Hannah mastered easily. Except here. She'd longed for this place and this feeling for months. She knew that nothing was solved, and the problems remained, but from here she could gain control and find s more realistic vision of them.

Hannah had no idea how long she leaned against the rock and let the peace fill her, she let her mind empty.

Feeling refreshed, Hannah began to notice that the wind was coming up a bit, making the tops of the trees sway and sigh louder and louder. She could see a bank of high clouds to the west. This was typical in these mountains, often they meant rain showers, accompanied by loud echoing thunder bouncing up and down through the valleys and across the mountain sides.

Hannah didn't want to leave this spot, but knew she was ready. The tranquility she found followed along as she made her way back to the cabin.

Chapter 13

August 15, 1902

Andriette quickly put on a different dress, a nicer blue frock with a tight waist and white collar and sleeves. She fussed for a few minutes with her hair when she noticed Nathan leaning against the doorpost watching her with a smile.

"You look beautiful," he said to her.

She didn't exactly agree, but she also knew this was a work outing, not a social one, so she put a comb in a small purse and turned to face him. "I'm ready."

To get to Dillon, they went back down their private road, across the creek and then turned right, up the mountain. The road was rough, and while it was only about two miles, it was a tough trip. They crossed the creek two more times, and wound through steep hills with dense forest all around before they came around a wide bend and got their first glimpse of Dillon. Of course, Nathan went to Dillon often and had told Andriette about it, but the actual sight of the town amazed her. Here, nearly at the top of the mountain range but nestled snuggly in a wide, alpine valley, was the beginning of a real town.

Andriette was amazed at the busy main street and the number of people and buildings she saw. This town looked somehow more cultured and urban than Battle. On her left as they approached was a row of buildings. At the center was a three-story structure with shiny glass windows and boardwalks out front. Across the street was the bank, the mercantile and the saloon with a wide boardwalk connecting them as well. Nathan smiled and watched Andriette's face as she took in the three-story Dillon Hotel and the large Mercantile. The saloon, the bank and the newspaper office as well as the livery stable, the land office, a café, and other buildings added to the businesses on Main Street. Construction sounds added percussion to the symphony of horses and people. Andriette could see at least five buildings being built.

Here was the hustle and bustle of any larger town she had ever seen. Andriette watched children and their mamas walk on the wooden boardwalk between the stores. Several men stood near the swinging doors of the saloon and talked as they watched Nathan pull the horses up and stop in front of the Mercantile.

Just then, a huge, thundering boom shook the ground and echoed through the valley. Andriette jumped and looked in fear at Nathan. He patted her leg and smiled. "You'll get used to that. The mine is only a mile up that draw, and they're working on sinking a new shaft. Dynamite really shakes the valley, doesn't it?"

"Andriette," Nathan said quietly, "I don't usually spend very much money here in Dillon, things are more expensive here than in Encampment. I am sure there are a few things we need though, so I will go into the Mercantile with you and introduce you to Elizabeth so you can do a little shopping. They do have fresh eggs and bacon here, and maybe you could find some fabric for the tablecloth you said you'd like to make. Get what we need. While you do that, I'll go find Allen Murphy, who is probably in the saloon, and get this lumber unloaded. It will take an hour or so. How about I meet you at the restaurant in the Dillon Hotel in about an hour? Is that alright with you?"

"It will be fun to do a little shopping, then, I may take a little walk around town and look around."

"That will be great."

As they walked into the mercantile, they attracted a bit of attention. The ladies of Dillon knew Nathan, and were highly interested in who was with him.

"Good morning Miss Elizabeth, how are you?" Nathan took off his hat and addressed a matronly woman of about forty who stood behind the counter.

"Well, Nathan Jameson, it has been a couple months since we saw you last, and look what you've brought with you!"

"Miss Elizabeth, this is my wife, Andriette. Andriette, this is Elizabeth Janing."

"Pleased to meet you," Andriette replied, but even before she could finish that short sentence, Elizabeth was around the counter and hugging her.

"A wife for Nathan! How wonderful, and how beautiful you are, too!"

Nathan made a discreet escape from the two ladies, and Andriette spent a pleasant time chatting. Soon, another customer entered the store. While Elizabeth was helping an older man choose some tools and other supplies, Andriette wandered around the store, looking at all the merchandise, marveling at how in a place like Dillon it was common to find a store that carried thread and buttons as well as chisels and fuses for blasting. As the man was paying Elizabeth, two women came in. Elizabeth said good-bye to the older gentleman then turned to the two other women who entered.

"Can you believe it, Nathan has a wife! Andriette, I'd like you to meet Mrs. Mary Nell Baker and Mrs. Claire Haynes."

Claire and Mary Nell were wives of men who worked at the mine in Rudefeha. Both women, who were about the same age as Andriette, had each been married for about two years and had lived in Dillon since spring just after the town started. Claire and her husband were from Iowa and Mary Nell and hers were from Colorado. Both couples came to

Dillon because of the promise of a good income for the miners.

The women both agreed that it was a risk to have their men deep underground each day. In some places the mine was 125 to 150 feet deep. To get to those depths the men climbed down steep shafts. The work in the mine was grueling, hard physical labor. Every so often there were accidents or small cave-ins, and men were killed or hurt, and so life in Dillon wasn't carefree.

As for being a woman in Dillon, there were good and bad. Mary Nell explained, "Most of the miners are unmarried, and they are a rowdy and tough-living breed of men. They spend a lot of their money and off time at the saloon, and get loud and obnoxious. The mine runs shifts, so it doesn't matter if it is day or evening or night, there are drunk and loud miners in town all day every day."

"Except Sunday," added Elizabeth, "Then the saloon is closed, and the miners are all tired and have headaches." The women laughed.

"I never walk through town alone at night, but overall no one bothers us." Both ladies were thankful that there were several women in town to be friends with and agreed that they would not be happy if they couldn't spend time in the company of other women.

They asked Andriette about her life in the forest, and while she talked about how peaceful and beautiful her solitary life with Nathan was, not one of the three women could understand how she could live so isolated.

The conversation turned to the coming winter. The residents described their plans for spending the winter in Dillon. They laughed at the two story privy that Mr. Dillon built out behind the boarding house. The plan was that when the snow got high, then the boarders would use the second story of the outhouse. Claire told how she'd just received a set of skis and looked forward to having her husband and Mary Nell teach her to use them.

"I got pretty good with my skis while we were in Telluride. The only way to get anywhere was to strap them on and go," Mary Nell explained.

The ladies talked about their plans of banding together with other wives to form a Ladies Society to meet, sew, chat and share a lunch. They invited Andriette to come and join them. Andriette was excited to have made new friends, but also knew that the trip wasn't one she probably could make often.

Andriette enjoyed the company of the women, but kept focused also on the time and what she'd come for. She did find some material for a tablecloth and some lace to edge it with that she thought wasn't too overpriced. She bought eggs and bacon and a tin of coffee for Nathan and a small bag of hard candy to share on the trip home this afternoon. She asked Elizabeth to wrap up her purchases and that they would pick them up on the way out of town.

The three wives parted eventually, saying goodbye in front of the mercantile. Mary Nell and Claire both lived in small cabins near each other on the hill overlooking Dillon's main street. They carried their daily purchases and went off up the hill together, after pointing out their homes to Andriette and offering warm invitations to visit. They also promised to get word to Andriette about the Ladies Society meetings when they were established.

Andriette walked up the street, conscious that she was alone, but not afraid or nervous. She liked watching the activity in town, and stopped to watch as a team of twenty mules pulling a large wagon made its way down the street. The muleteer's hands were full with forty straps, the reins for the rig, and he kept a close eye on the traffic and people he approached. He was dusty and haggard looking, but probably not much older than Nathan. She stood and stared, marveling at how he could so adeptly control the team.

"Amazing feat, isn't it? To make twenty mules all go in the same direction."

Andriette turned to look at the man beside her. He was a portly gentleman probably in his mid-fifties. He wore a dark suit made of expensive material. The jacket was finely tailored and unbuttoned, revealing a matching vest over a crisp white shirt. The gold chain leading to the vest pocket could only lead to an expensive watch.

The man obviously was rich, but his face was open and honest, and she felt at once at ease and comfortable.

"I'm Malachi Dillon, Ma'am," he smiled and tipped his hat.

"It's nice to meet you, Mr. Dillon, I'm Andriette Jameson."

"Jameson is it? Are you Nathan's new bride then?"

She stammered, "Yes, you know Nathan?"

"Know Nathan? Of course! He helped build my boarding house! I don't think we'd have ever gotten it built without Nathan's skill and his sweet mother's supplies."

Andriette knew that Nathan had worked as a carpenter here, but didn't know he'd helped build the boarding house.

"I saw Nathan a few minutes ago, he and Allan Murphy were unloading a wagon. May I invite you to have tea with me at the Hotel?" He offered Andriette his arm.

"That would be wonderful," she answered and took his arm. "Nathan and I arranged to meet here for lunch, in fact."

They walked the boardwalk past the bank and entered the Dillon Hotel. On the outside, the hotel rose three stories of windows looking out over Main Street. The building was made of logs, but the pounded tin veneer made it look brick. Inside, the lobby was shiny and clean. The walls were lacquered logs, giving the wide room a rich feel. Off to the left was the reception desk backed by a wall full of shelves and cubbies for guest mail and messages. The restaurant was to the right, through a wide arched opening. A corridor led towards the back, ending in swinging doors that clearly opened to the saloon.

Mr. Dillon indicated a table by the window, and held the chair for Andriette as she sat down.

"It is clear that the hotel is named for you, Mr. Dillon, is the town named for you as well?"

Dillon chuckled good naturedly. "Yes, I started this town just six months ago. You see, Mrs. Jameson, I am the son of a tavern keeper, and came west with the idea to follow in my father's business. I knew both Haggarty and Ferris and had business dealings with Jim Rumsey and worked for a little while up at the Rudefeha mine for them. It was my intent all the time to build a saloon nearby so the miners could have a drink and relax after a hard shift of working. I saved up what I needed to get started, quit work at the mine and ordered some lumber to begin building. When those old boys found out my intent, they threw a fit. They were adamant that there would be no bar and no alcohol anywhere near their mine.

"I moved my lumber down the mountain a mile, staked a claim for the land so there would not be anyone to tell me what I could and couldn't do, and built the saloon and a boardinghouse."

"Is business good, then?"

Again he smiled. "I don't charge anyone to stay at the boardinghouse as long as they do their drinking at my saloon."

"That's quite a story, Mr. Dillon. Are you still friends with the men who own the mine?"

"Our relations were strained for a time, but all is well now."

"The mine must be very successful. Does everyone who lives here have a connection to the mine?"

"In one way or another, about all the people in my town of Dillon are connected to the mine or supplying the mine. The exception to that are the sheepherders. In the summer, ranchers from down on the plains bring their sheep up here to graze. The men who herd them are Basques, a hardy lot they are."

"The town is much larger than I expected it to be," Andriette admitted. "Is there a sheriff?"

"No, the Marshall from Encampment comes up every so often, and he'd be the one to handle anything serious that happens here, but mostly we govern and police ourselves. Certainly there is a fight or two once in a while in the saloon between miners that drink a bit more than they should. My barkeeps are good at taking care of things before they turn into big trouble. The only serious trouble we have is an ongoing feud between the miners and the sheepherders."

"What causes the friction between the two groups?"

Dillon fidgeted in his chair. "Let's just say they don't always get along," he answered.

Andriette could tell he was uncomfortable so she let the subject drop.

"Are you aware that Dillon will soon have its own newspaper, Mrs. Jameson?"

"No, I didn't know that," she answered.

"Yes, the newspaper office is just completed. We're waiting on the printing press and supplies. Hopefully the newspaper will begin printing before the end of the year. We're eager and enthused about our *Dillon DoubleJack*. Grant Jones is the owner, print setter, publisher and writer. He's a dynamic and talented young man."

Andriette sipped her tea and looked around. It was impressive that all this was only six months old.

"I'm interested to know about the new Mrs. Jameson. May I ask how you and Nathan met?"

Andriette sat her cup down and hesitated. She was shy to share their story, but Mr. Dillon seemed truly interested. "When Nathan was young in Encampment, there was a family, the Clements, who lived close by. Nathan and Andrew Clement were good pals. Andrew's father moved the family to Council Bluffs, Iowa during the drought here about ten years ago, but the families kept in touch. The Clements were my next door neighbors. As a teen, Andrew did odd jobs for my aunts and befriended me. Andrew is a great story teller, and he told me lots of boyhood stories of himself and his friend Nathan. Two years ago, at Andrew's urging, Nathan and I began writing to one another."

"Oh, so it seems you've had a long courtship."

"It certainly didn't start as a courtship, but it didn't take very long to discover that we both see the world similarly. Eventually I realized that I respected and admired him for the sincere way he lived." Andriette smiled. "It took Nathan a bit longer to decide that it was mutual. Then we began to make plans for a visit. Soon, it was clear to both of us that a visit wasn't enough, and he wrote to ask me to marry him."

Dillon met her eyes and smiled. She saw nothing there but kindness. "I wish you both the best. I think the world of Nathan, and you are a charming young woman."

Andriette was pleased and relieved. She glanced out the window to see Nathan making his way down the boardwalk. He smiled broadly as he entered and saw Andriette. He greeted Dillon with a handshake.

"I should have assumed you'd find a way to meet my wife," Nathan teased.

"We've enjoyed a pleasant chat. It's about time you settled down with someone, and Andriette is just lovely."

The three had a pleasant conversation over a delicious lunch. Andriette enjoyed the attention of her husband as well as the company of Mr. Dillon. "Mrs. Jameson," Mr. Dillon put his hand out to Andriette. "It has been delightful to meet you, and I hope that you will come back soon and often. I have a meeting at the bank that I must attend, so I will take your leave."

They finished their good-byes and watched him leave. Nathan told her that the delivery was fine and asked about her time alone in Dillon. She told him about meeting the ladies at the mercantile and that she'd like to sometime come in to Dillon to attend a Ladies Society meeting.

"That sounds like a great idea. I worry that you'll get too lonely to want to stay with me," Nathan responded.

"Nathan, that isn't anything you should worry about. I love being in the forest in our home with you."

"I just don't want you to ever want anything you don't have, Andriette." Nathan locked his eyes on hers for a moment.

They finished their lunch and found that Mr. Dillon had picked up the bill for them. "He seems like such a nice man," Andriette commented as they were leaving the table.

"He is a shrewd businessman, and he owns most of this town's land and several of the businesses as well as several mining claims in the area. You are right, he is a nice man." Nathan finished his comment as they made their way through the tables and into the lobby of the Hotel. "I left the wagon at the livery. We can walk over to the Mercantile and pick up your packages, then head back to the wagon."

He held the door for her and she walked through. Two women were approaching, so he held the door for them to enter.

"Well look, Marci, it's Nathan!" said the taller of the two. She threaded her arm through Nathan's and pulled him tightly to her side. "It's been so long since we've seen you I thought you'd left the mountains."

Nathan was instantly red in the face and flustered. He disengaged himself from her and stepped away, reaching for Andriette's hand at the same time.

"Um, uh, Andriette, I'd like you to meet two, um, ladies who live here in Dillon. This is Marci and this is Catherine. Ladies, this is my wife, Andriette."

Andriette had never seen Nathan so unsure of himself. The ladies remained calm but the atmosphere changed rapidly from one of amusement and lightness to cool.

Andriette took a breath and reached her hand out. "Pleased to meet you both." She shook hands with Marci, and offered a hand to Catherine, who stared hard at Andriette and did not move.

"I'm sure," she finally answered. Then she walked away.

Andriette didn't know what to think about the encounter.

Nathan put his arm around her waist and they walked to the Mercantile in silence. Andriette found her packages neatly bundled. Elizabeth handed them to Andriette as Nathan paid her and thanked her. He carried the parcels and they made their way to the livery walking side by side.

They talked a little but mostly the silence continued after they were on the wagon and headed home. Andriette was lost in thought. She remembered fondly Mary Nell and Claire and their invitation to the Ladies Society. She hoped that it could be worked out that she could go to the meetings sometimes. She thought about the charming Mr. Dillon and their lovely lunch.

Her thoughts kept returning, however, to the encounter with the ladies in front of the Hotel. Both women were beautiful. They were richly dressed, though perhaps overly so for the middle of the day. Both wore discreet make-up on their eyes, cheeks and lips. Andriette began to compare herself to them, she with her plain face and simple cotton dress. She was certain that there had been something between Catherine and Nathan. She was so glad to see him and shut down so quickly when he'd introduced Andriette to them. Andriette began to wonder at the relationship. She felt outclassed and outdone by Catherine, and her worries began to grow with each moment that Nathan stayed quiet.

Lord, she prayed. *I think I am jealous and I need your help. This jealously has made me a little mad at Nathan and has made me doubt myself. The meeting with those ladies put a damper on a very nice and special day. Lord, keep my temper and my worries under control and help me to understand this situation better before I say anything mean or hurtful.*

Just before the road crossed the Haggarty Creek the first time down the mountain, Nathan pulled the wagon off the road a bit into a small meadow and set the brake. He got down then turned and reached a hand up. "Will you take a little walk with me?"

She took his hand and got down from the wagon. They walked across the meadow to a large aspen tree. Nathan stopped. They stood for several moments, looking at each other. Andriette couldn't read Nathan's thoughts, and she felt a little frightened about what he was going to say. Finally, he reached out and took her hand and began.

"Andriette, I want you to know that I love you and I am happy." It was clear he had more to say, but this was what Andriette needed to hear most. She burst into tears.

Nathan was at a loss. He wasn't sure what to do or what the tears meant. He held her closely against him and waited. Andriette got herself together quickly, then, and looked up at him. "Catherine seemed so glad to see you and was so familiar with you. Did you court her? She is very attractive, are you sorry you are married to me?"

Nathan looked shocked. He realized then that Andriette hadn't completely understood the situation. "No, I never courted her. Andri, she's not the kind of woman a fellow would court. She works at the saloon, she and Marci and several other women."

"Works at the saloon?" Andriette was having trouble absorbing this new information.

"Yes, she, um, she brings drinks and is paid to be nice to the men at the saloon."

The full meaning of what Nathan was telling her finally sunk in. "Nathan, you're telling me that those two ladies sell themselves? Oh Nathan, she was so glad to see you, have you…?"

Nathan saw that now she understood fully. "No, Andri. When I worked in Dillon, and even afterwards when I'd go into town, I'd stop in at the saloon. Sometimes I'd have a drink or two and relax. Catherine was always there, and she'd flirt with me. It became a contest between us to see if I'd give in to her."

"So you haven't ever been with…"

"No! I know most men don't feel the way I do, but I think men should stay pure for marriage, too. Andriette, I have never had a relationship with anyone but you. I am thankful for that, because what we have is special, and God given, and I'm really glad that there is nothing in my past actions that would take away from our marriage in any way."

Andriette cried again then, in relief and in gratitude for Nathan and for God's leading him even before he knew her. They stood for a long time in the meadow, just holding on to each other.

When they were moving down the road again, Andriette remembered her conversation with Malachi Dillon. "Nathan, Mr. Dillon said that there was sometimes trouble between the sheepherders and the miners in Dillon. What is the problem?"

Nathan turned his head sharply to look at Andriette, then threw back his head and laughed merrily. "I'm sorry Andri, but you couldn't have timed that question any better." He chuckled again and went on. "The trouble is that sheep have ticks, and sheepherders often carry those ticks on their clothes and persons. Sometimes, those ticks get left in certain beds in Dillon. Later, miners might get bitten by those ticks when they frequent those same beds."

Andriette felt her face getting warm as she understood what Nathan was telling her. He laughed again and so did she.

Chapter 14

August 21, 2007

It's Wednesday already, the days are going so quickly. It was Hannah's first thought the next morning. She sighed as the 'real world' loomed up at her. She'd planned to get a fairly early start on Saturday morning so that she'd be home in time to do a load or two of laundry in the evening and also have a lazy Sunday in her apartment and get ready for work on Monday. Now she was reconsidering. If she left on Sunday, she'd still have plenty of time to get back to Denver.

She felt discouraged. She'd wanted the forest and the cabin visit to fix everything and give her clarity and peace. She did feel better, but she was clueless about how to deal with her trials at work, and she still felt alone and abandoned.

She padded downstairs to the stove and put on the kettle for tea. While the kettle was heating, Hannah looked at the closed door of her father's room. "Today is the day." Hannah said it out loud, trying to work up to the task ahead of her. When the tea kettle whistled, she poured herself a cup, squared her shoulders and entered the room. Tears immediately filled her eyes as she looked from the doorway. Dad used this room both for reading and sleeping. To the right was a closet door. Hannah knew that she'd find Dad's cabin jackets and boots and also a porta potty. It hardly ever got used, except for during rainy nights, or on the rare occasions her mom came up. Next to the closet was the bed, flanked by two antique chairs her mother found at an auction. These served as the bedside tables. The bed was covered with a quilt Hannah's mom made for her dad when they were first married. It was faded blue denim, the pieces cut from old worn out jeans of Dad's. On each of the bedside chairs were framed pictures. The one to the left was of Hannah's parents, smiling with their arms around one another. The picture on the right was of Hannah at six years old, smiling with a grin showing gaps where her two front baby teeth used to be. Hannah smiled back at the little girl. She remembered the day Dad took that shot. They ate s'mores for breakfast, something only allowed on trips to the cabin, and then played in the creek.

Hannah sat down on the bed, turning to look at the other wall of the bedroom. The small window at the center of the room was encased by shelves which held many books in addition to rocks and souvenirs of their mountain explorations. One shelf held a whiskey bottle, purpled with age, they found near the creek. Another shelf held a bottle with "The Great Dr. Kilmer's Swamp Root Kidney Liver & Bladder Cure" in raised letters on the glass. Nearby sat a key to the Dillon Hotel and a stack of coins that read "Good for 12 ½ c in trade at the bar" on one side and "Dillon Saloon" on the other.

An archival box filled with a stack of assorted copies of the *Dillon DoubleJack* and the *Encampment Echo* filled one shelf. Dad loved to read the newspaper with his morning coffee, and both he and Hannah enjoyed randomly choosing a newspaper, from 1898 or 1909 or any time in between to read. Often, Dad read her articles from the papers and they discussed them. As she grew up, Hannah came to understand that those morning reads were actually the study of history in its finest form. The people and events were real and vibrant to her, even though they happened nearly a hundred years ago. The line between past and present sometimes blurred for her while she was at the cabin. She fully expected sometimes to hike to Dillon and see it in its glory. Occasionally a sound, perhaps from a passing car on the highway would echo in her imagination like the tramway carrying ore buckets over the mountain.

She wasn't sure how long she'd sat on Dad's bed, looking at the shelves full of trinkets and books, but in the interim, the tears she'd shed on entering the room dried up to be replaced by a soft smile, both on her face and in her heart.

Finally, she got up and walked to the small desk in the corner. She ran her finger over the smooth wood top, then touched the items laying there: a feather from a hawk, two Bic pens and a small spiral notebook. She recognized these as common accessories on the desk. Dad often picked up interesting rocks or other treasures that caught his eye. He always carried with him a notebook and pen, so that if he got an idea he could jot it down so as not to forget. Beside these familiar trappings sat a beautiful wooden box. About the size of small shoebox, the rich deep wood tones, the worn edges and few nicks and scratches gave her the impression that it was old. Hannah ran her hand over the carved top's intricately detailed mountain scene. The years had worn some of the detail to mere hints. She wondered where the small chest came from and reached to pick it up and investigate what was inside when her eyes and hands came to a complete halt. She felt in a heartbeat that the world stood still as she stared at the envelope on the desk. "To Hannah" was written in Dad's careful handwriting.

"Oh Dad," Hannah's tears welled again. She knew then that what she'd found was what she'd come for.

Chapter 15

September 5, 1902

Fall is here thought Andriette as she sat enjoying the clear afternoon. The meadow was still beautiful; the warmth of the rock against her back was welcome due to the crispness of the morning air. She sat there for about half an hour, praying and reflecting on her life. She knew that they would need to decide soon whether to stay in the mountains for the winter or go to Encampment. She shared Nathan's love for the home they shared in the mountains, and neither of them was anxious to give up their solitude for living in a city and sharing a home with Lillian. She was concerned, though, with the coming winter.

"Winter up this high in the mountains is hard, Andri," Nathan brought up the discussion last night at dinner. "The snow gets deep here. Last winter I dug out after a storm, and when I finally got out, all I could see of the house was the top few feet of roof. The snow really packs down in here." He described the bitter cold and the feeling of being trapped that he'd fought. "They call it cabin fever."

Andriette wasn't sure she'd like that trapped feeling, but she didn't want to let Nathan down if he wanted to stay.

Lord I am praying for guidance here. Neither Nathan nor I seem to know what the best choice is. This is our home, and we don't really want to leave for the winter, but I am a little - no Lord - a lot scared about spending the winter up here. Dear Father, please direct us. She sat in silence for a few minutes and then finished her prayer. *Lord, thank you for your love for us. Thy will be done on this. And Lord, thank you for this rock and this sanctuary you have given me. Bless anyone who ever sits here. Help them to feel and be as safe as I feel here.*

Andriette opened her eyes and started to get up when a movement on the other side of the meadow caught her eye. She froze and watched as a mountain lion moved out of the trees and stood at the edge of the meadow. The cat was beautiful. Its body was about six feet long and it stood about two and a half feet high at the shoulder. It was rich tan in color with sleek dark markings on its face. It walked gracefully a bit farther into the meadow and stopped, looked around and then directly at Andriette. They stayed that way for a few heartbeats. Andriette was too awed and frightened to even breathe, the cat was sizing her up. They locked eyes, and Andriette knew that the cat saw her and was considering its next move when a movement near the cat caught Andriette's eye. Two lion cubs bounded into the meadow, chasing one another and playing. They were miniature versions of their mother, each about the size of a large house cat. Andriette looked away for a moment from the mother, then, to watch the cubs play. She smiled at their playfulness and at their rich beauty. Then she looked back at the mama, realizing that she was in clear danger. A female mountain lion would be deadly if protecting her cubs. *Lord!* Was all she could think of to pray.

The mama lion didn't move a muscle and continued to stare at Andriette. Finally, she gave a low growl and turned away. She bounded off into the woods, her cubs, now alert to her and obeying her signal, followed. Just like that they were gone.

Andriette reminded herself to breathe once again. The encounter lasted less than a minute, but seemed so much longer. Her heart was pounding from the fear and danger, but also from the excitement of having been blessed with seeing such an amazing animal. She couldn't wait to tell Nathan.

Andriette hurried down the hillside to the sawmill. Nathan was working hard to finish the latest load of lumber and get it delivered before the snow closed the road to travel. He looked up and saw her coming. He hugged her and then listened to her tell him about the mountain lion and her cubs. Just as she was finishing her story, a rider approached. It was Bart Dooley. He was a courier between Encampment and the Rudefeha mine, and once in a while he'd stop by their house for a rest or to deliver a letter or small package from Lillian. There was regular mail service between Dillon and Encampment, but no real service to their house in the mountains. Everyone knew, though, that Bart would be willing to carry something if he could. Andriette kept up a regular correspondence with Lillian through the summer thanks to Bart.

After greetings all around, Nathan invited Bart in for some dinner. He declined the offer, but handed over a letter. "I am in a hurry to get some papers up to the mine, so I can't stay today. Miss Abby asked me to get this to you right away, though."

They thanked Bart and asked him to stop by on his way back down to Encampment the next day, to pick up a return letter for Lillian. He agreed and they saw him off, then sat down on a log side by side to read the letter. Abby wrote to say that Lillian was ill. She had come down with influenza and was very sick. It seemed that the worst was over and she was almost certainly going to be all right, but a full recovery would take quite a while. Nathan read Abby's last sentences aloud. "Nathan, I know that you really don't want to move down here for the winter, but Mother is going to need help while she recuperates. I can't stay at the store all day and I can't do her housework and my own, with the baby so small. We need you and Andriette."

They sat on a log for a few minutes discussing the situation. Nathan agreed that they needed to go to Encampment. He asked Andriette to write back to Abby and tell her that they would be coming down the mountain within the next two weeks.

With the decision made, they both went to work getting ready to move for the winter. Andriette helped Nathan at the sawmill, then they both worked together to get the cabin ready. Nathan checked the shutters for the windows and attached them to the outside of the cabin, closing them securely. They were busy, but even so Andriette found time every day to walk up to the meadow and spend a few minutes at her rock. The day before they were to leave the air was very cold and the sky was overcast. Andriette sat, wrapped in her coat, with her back to the rock when Nathan came into view.

"I always know you'll be here if you aren't at the cabin," he teased. "May I join you?"

"Of course," she answered and scooted over to make room. They sat for a few minutes in the comfortable quiet of the forest. "It's funny how much I love this spot. I feel so at home in the mountains with you, and this spot is so special."

They sat, holding hands, and talked about the events of the summer. They had grown very close in the three months since they'd first met in Rawlins, and they took time that morning to reflect on the blessings and challenges they faced in that time. Both knew that their marriage was strong and that God directed them to each other.

"We need to get an early start in the morning. I am hoping we can make Encampment in one day on this trip. The wagon won't be loaded very heavily and once we reach Battle, it is mostly downhill. It may be a long, cold day, though. Also, let's be sure to take along some extra food and supplies so that if the weather gets bad, we can make camp if we need to."

After a few more quiet moments, during which Andriette prayed for the trip and the coming winter, they slowly made their way back to the cabin.

They awoke early the next morning and were greeted by a world under a blanket of snow. The clouds were breaking up a bit, though, so they knew that the storm was passed and they could safely start out. Nathan was correct, the day was long and cold. They stopped for a brief rest in Battle to say hello to Pearl. They relaxed with a cup of hot coffee to warm them before continuing the trip.

Nathan secretly wondered if Abby hadn't exaggerated Lillian's illness as a ploy to get them to move down the mountain. It was clear, though, that the letter actually understated Lillian's illness when they arrived at her house in Encampment.

Andriette hugged the woman and then stepped back to look at her. She was pale and had dark circles under her eyes. She was much thinner and seemed fragile. Both Nathan and Andriette were thankful that they had come.

Chapter 16

August 21, 2007

Dearest Hannah,

I hope that it won't take you long after I am gone to make your way to the cabin, so I am leaving this for you here, where we have spent so many happy hours and days. I need you to hear from me that every moment I spent with you, every moment, brought me joy. Now, I know that you have been angry with me for not fighting this old cancer more. Our last few discussions have been heated. Don't let yourself feel guilty for that, I heard loud and clear in your arguing how much you love me. Don't let yourself spend too much more time being mad at me either, please. Anger is such a waste of time. Hannah, it is my time to go. I feel really sure that life doesn't end here and that I will see you and your mom again. I am ready for this new journey.

One more thing I am convinced of is that God's definition of time is different from ours, so even when I am gone, don't think for a minute that I am not praying for you and loving you.

You are strong and smart and beautiful and I love you dearly. Think carefully about your life, then live it with abandon.

Love forever,

Dad

P.S. I found a treasure for you to enjoy. The new owners of that stone house in Encampment were doing some renovations and found this in the cellar. They told Bob Warren at the store about it. He mentioned it to me and I contacted them. They were happy to pass it on to someone who was interested in "that sort of thing". I did a little research. I can't prove it for sure, but I think the box may have originally come from the cabin on our land.

Chapter 17

May 1, 1903

Winter passed happily. Nathan spent his days at the store, taking charge of its day to day management. He and Lillian spent an evening or two a week sitting together at the kitchen table going over the accounts and ordering merchandise. Lillian was patient in teaching him about the business and its inner workings, and Nathan learned quickly. She was grateful for his help and for the ideas he shared for how to make the store run even better.

During the day, Andriette cooked and cleaned and became the de facto lady of the house while Lillian recovered. They had an amiable relationship and instead of feeling as if Andriette was taking over, Lillian only felt thankful for the energy and heart of the woman who was her son's wife. They enjoyed each other's company. As the Spring progressed, Lillian regained her strength and began sharing and then taking back over the household work. By March, Lillian was her normal self again and she shared jam recipes and the three women worked on a quilt together.

Abby came over nearly every day to see them and to let Harrison spend time with his Grandma and aunt. He was a sweet baby, quickly growing into being a rowdy little boy. He entertained the three women with his antics, and they spent many pleasant afternoons together. On Sundays Mark and Abby and Harrison would come for a family dinner. When

Lillian was ready, the family went to church together on Sunday mornings. Andriette's family never worshipped together, so Sundays became extra special for her.

The entire town of Encampment was excited about the progress being made on the tramway. The smelter in Encampment closed down for most of the winter, partly due to a temporary dip in copper prices, but mostly so that the men who usually worked there could help in building the tram. Mark spent many nights away as he helped to build transfer station number two up near Cow Creek. Estimates were that the tram would be complete and in service by the end of June.

As spring approached, Andriette could tell that Nathan was getting anxious. He also seemed to be a bit distanced from her. She watched him closely, then, trying to figure out what was on his mind. Several times he was short with her and her concern grew. She didn't think Lillian or Abby noticed anything, but she was worried.

All day he seemed even more tense than usual. The weather was warm and clear, snow was melting in the valley though the mountains were still a white wall to the west. At dinner, Lillian and Andriette chatted about their day and laughingly told him about finishing a quilt earlier that afternoon.

"I've ordered some new material for the wedding ring quilt we will make next," Lillian commented.

Nathan's eyes were stormy. He said nothing for the rest of the meal and excused himself quickly to go out to the barn. This time, Lillian did notice.

"Would you mind cleaning up dinner by yourself tonight, Lillian? I'd like to go be with Nathan," Andriette said to her quietly.

"I think that's a good idea, Dear, you go ahead." Lillian was a bit worried as well.

Andriette found Nathan in the barn working on the buckboard. He didn't look up when she entered, but she knew that he'd heard her come in. She stood for a while and watched as he worked on one wheel. He appeared to finish what he was doing and stood up, wiping the axle grease from his hands with a rag. "There, now the wheels are all greased and the buckboard is ready to go, if we decide we need it." There was anger in his voice.

Andriette prayed. *Lord, I am not sure what is happening here. Give me wisdom to understand Nathan's mood.* She walked closer to him and took his hand. He started to withdraw, but she held on and he relaxed.

"Nathan, what have I done that has upset you?"

He did pull away then, and answered roughly, "Not a thing." It was clear he didn't mean what he'd said.

"Really, I need to know what is bothering you so that we can work it out." Her voice was a bit louder than she'd intended, her frustration showing.

"Andriette, go back in the house. I'm sure you and Mother have some fun and exciting plan or project to work on. Just let me be."

"Nathan, are you upset because your mother and I are getting along so well?"

"No Andriette, I'm not upset at all." He was yelling now. "I love the idea that my wife is such good friends with my mother that she won't ever want to go back to our home. I love it that you have plans and have made preparations for living here when it is time we should be preparing to go back to the mountains and I love it that I am about to have to choose between the life I've made for us in the mountains and the woman I love!"

His voice echoed in their minds and off the barn walls.

Andriette tried to be calm but succeeded only partly. Nathan had never yelled at her before, she wasn't used to seeing him angry. She wanted to calm him down and solve the situation, but at the same time she was angry at him for not trusting her more. "Nathan Jameson, you are being irrational." Her voice was very quiet. She was careful to enunciate every word clearly. Her anger became very apparent to Nathan in the deliberateness of her quiet response.

"Throughout this winter, Lillian and I have continued a running conversation about her fears of you being alone in the mountains, both in the summer and the winter. I believe that I have now convinced her that we are a strong and able partnership. She feels very confident that we are happy, that you are happy, and that staying in the mountains isn't nearly as big a problem for the two of us as for just you."

Nathan started to speak, the anger quickly draining from his eyes and face, but Andriette put up her hand to stop him and continued. "The quilt we finished today is extra thick so that we will be warm next winter when we stay in the mountains. If you'll look behind you in the corner, you will see the stack of boxes I have begun packing of things I feel we need to take home with us. In that stack are things like new towels, more heavy socks for you and for me, and a new pair of boots Lillian gave me so that my feet stay dry in the snow. There are also two pairs of skis, one for you and one for me that we found in the attic and thought might be helpful.

"Furthermore, Sir, you will find in that box on the top packets of seeds so that I can plant a garden of more than tomatoes and potatoes this year. I was thinking that maybe you'd appreciate carrots and beans and peas for your suppers next winter. The box next to it has jars for canning. I am ready to go home any time you say. The only choice you have to make is what day we leave."

Nathan was speechless. He was sorry he'd been angry and sorry he'd doubted her. He felt sheepish and ashamed that he'd yelled. Andriette could see it in his eyes and he knew it. "Well Woman," he smiled and continued, now in mock seriousness. "It's about time you did something useful. The snow is still too deep for travel. We'll watch the run-off and the weather. We need to start buying supplies at the Mercantile. I'd love to go home within the next few weeks."

They embraced then, and let all the remnants of their fight slough off. Nathan kissed her and held her tightly. Quietly he apologized. "Andriette, I love you so much. You have been so dear to Mother, and you two have gotten along so well. I truly have been afraid that you'd never want to go back up into the mountains."

"I'll admit I have enjoyed being here. I don't remember my mother. My family was always so formal and stilted with one another. Being with a family, being a part of this family, has been an amazing blessing to me, Nathan. I will always cherish the memories of this winter. I love you. I can't wait to go home and live our simple life in the mountains."

Chapter 18

August 21, 2007

Hannah read the letter over and over, hearing her dad's voice each time. Her tears dried and what remained was a growing strength from knowing that her dad truly understood her and loved her, even at her worst. His confidence in her buoyed her. Finally, she folded the letter and carefully placed it inside the envelope, thinking about dad's concept of God being above time. She was strengthened by a new insight into what omnipotence means. She laid the letter on the desk next to the treasure box, deciding that she would wait to explore its contents later.

She looked around the room. There were things that needed doing. Now she had the strength to do them. She gathered some grocery sacks from the kitchen cabinet and began sorting through her Dad's cabin clothes, shoes and boots. She saved a couple flannel shirts that would fit her and a heavy jacket, the rest she folded and put in the sacks so she could drop them off at the homeless shelter near her apartment. Then she brought down her belongings from the loft, moving them lovingly into her new room.

I need a walk in the trees, Hannah told herself when she finished. She grabbed her backpack and camera, filled her water bottle and threw in a bag of peanuts then headed for the front porch. She decided to work her way towards the meadow by the old cabin, and stepped off the porch. As she did, she tuned in to the sound of a motor. Thinking that it sounded nearer than the highway, Hannah angled towards the front gate of the property. A ways off she could see an old pickup parked on the other side of the closed gate. Curious, she quickened her pace and walked over.

"Hello," she called as she approached the gate.

The man leaned against the tailgate at the back of the pickup. Hearing her voice, he turned around and came towards her. He was her height or a bit taller, with shoulder length dishwater blond hair and a mustache. He was wearing a tight blue tee shirt that showed off his muscular chest and arms. His jeans were slung low on his hips with a hole in one knee. He stared at Hannah, but didn't answer.

"May I help you?" She tried again.

He continued to stare for a second or two more, then answered in a soft, quiet voice, "No Ma'am, I was just takin' a break and enjoying the mornin'. You live here?"

"We have a cabin up the ridge," Hannah cautiously answered. "Where are you headed?"

Again, a pause before he answered, but then a quick smile. "Oh, here and there, I'm meeting someone nearby. We're scouting out hunting spots for the fall."

"This gate marks the beginning of private property. The next turnoff down the road is access to forest service land."

"I'm thinkin' it looks like a good hunting area." His eyes locked on hers and didn't stray.

"As I said, it is private land, and we don't allow hunting."

"Sure is an isolated part of the forest."

"It's a bit off the beaten path. The ruggedness makes it even more beautiful." Hannah was eager to end the conversation. "I was just making sure that you weren't having car trouble or something. I'll leave you to get on your way," Hannah began to walk away.

"Have a good one," the man answered. She'd only taken a few steps when she heard the door slam and the engine start. As the engine noise retreated, Hannah thought about the man. He looked a bit familiar, but she was sure she'd never met him before. He could be handsome if he cleaned up, Hannah thought as she walked away, but there was something about him that made her a little uncomfortable.

She put the encounter out of her mind and headed up hill. She wanted to take some pictures of the wildflowers she'd seen in the meadow above the old cabin. She walked leisurely, enjoying the warmth of the day and the beauty around her. Squirrels and birds chirped and sang an irregular song overhead. She walked through the trees to the old cabin. Certainly there was once a clearing here, but in the years since the cabin was last lived in, the trees had reclaimed it. She strolled around the cabin, wondering again about the people who lived here. This was someone's home. She and Dad tried to research who had owned this place, but weren't able to find anything. She thought of Dad's letter again, and especially the postscript. She smiled at the memory of the times she and Dad had speculated on the kind of people who lived here. She liked to think that maybe they were robbers or bandits that used the cabin as a getaway after a train heist. Her dad, always the practical historian, would remind her that outlaws would have had little use for the china and crockery they found broken shards of, and that rarely did desperados have need of a boiler like the one that sat near the house. Maybe the treasure box would answer some of their questions.

Hannah walked over to the boiler as she looked around. It was huge and heavy, made of cast iron, it was about twelve feet long and four feet high. The years of erosion and deep snow had toppled it off its legs, so it rested now on one side. Hannah scrambled up and sat on top. She tried imagining it being brought here with a mule team wagon. *People then must have been much tougher than we are now,* she thought. *I can't imagine how hard life would have been living out here summer and winter.*

After a rest and a drink of water, Hannah headed up the slope to the meadow. She spent an hour or more snapping close ups of flowers. Patience rewarded her with several really fine shots of butterflies and bees as they helped themselves to the bounty the flowers offered them. Finally, she gathered her backpack and started downhill. She stopped for a minute at the big rock at the edge of the meadow. She put her hand on it and lingered. She always felt such peace here. *I'm still a little mad at you, God,* Hannah prayed. *But thanks for this day and this place.*

Chapter 19

June 13, 1903

Just a week after they'd arrived home, Nathan returned from a delivery trip to Dillon.

"Hello the house," he called as he rode in. "Andriette, where are you?"

Andriette wiped the dirt from her hands on her apron. She surveyed the enlarged garden she'd just finished planting. She admired her rows for beans, peas and carrots next to several hills of potatoes and three strong tomato plants.

"I'm here. Is everything okay?"

He got down off the buckboard and hugged her. He held her closely and kissed the top of her forehead. "I bought you a present in town, today," he began. "I was talking to Elizabeth Janing at the Mercantile. She asked about you and said that the ladies would really enjoy it if you'd come to the Ladies Society meetings. That started me to thinking. You could go to Dillon more often and attend those meetings if you had a horse to ride other than these big old Morgans we've got. Then, when I met with Allen Murphy to deliver the lumber, he mentioned that he just got a really gentle saddle horse he'd like to sell."

"You bought me a horse?"

"She's a mare, named Daisy."

"You bought me horse?" She knew she was sounding like a ninny, but couldn't help herself. Being able to go to

Dillon by herself was a good idea, but she hadn't been on horseback for a long time. They walked to the back of the wagon, where the mare was tied. She was chestnut brown with soft, dewy eyes and dark main and tail.

"Nathan, she's beautiful!"

"I never asked if you could ride, but I can teach you."

"I used to ride when I was young. A school chum who lived on the outskirts of town invited me out to her house in the summer and we would ride. I can probably handle her."

"The saddle that came with her is a regular saddle. I could get you a side-saddle if you'd rather?"

"No, side-saddle is really uncomfortable and hard on your back. I'd rather ride astride. Nathan, thank you! Can we afford this?"

"Allen made me a good deal, so yes, we can."

Nathan also handed her a letter from Lillian. "I picked this up from Bart this morning." They sat down and read it together. Most of the letter was filled with a description of the celebration in Encampment on June ninth. The first bucket of copper ore arrived in Encampment on a tramway bucket about noon. "The whole town was there, cheering and waving flags. One of the miners climbed up on a tower on the outskirts of town to watch for the first full bucket. He got so excited when he saw the ore, he jumped right on and rode the bucket all the way through town in to the smelter. People ran along underneath, cheering and hollering." Lillian went on to add that the tram is now running all night and day, and that she thought it would take some getting used to listening to the sound of the machinery.

Nathan told Andriette news about the tram. "Now that it is finished, there are 370 towers. Some of them are only ten feet tall, others are up to seventeen feet tall. There are also sixteen tension stations to keep it all running. The highest the cables get off the ground is 250 feet, and there is one place over by Cow Creek that spans 2,200 feet. There are 985 ore buckets that can carry 750 to1000 pounds each."

Andriette was awed. "What makes it run?"

"Gravity mostly. There are three stations that can add power from steam."

"I'm impressed. It's a marvel of technology."

"That's for sure. And at fifteen and three quarters miles long, they say it's the longest aerial tramway in the world."

The rest of June flew by. Andriette tended her garden and the house and helped Nathan at the saw mill. She rode the three miles into Dillon nearly every week to attend Ladies Society meetings and pick up a few supplies while she was there. Each outing was special. The first meeting was punctuated by the news that Claire, her first friend in Dillon, was expecting.

On a bright morning at the end of the first week in July, Andriette looked around as she stepped out of the cabin. She was a bit tired from the big day she and Nathan had yesterday. As she stood at the door of the cabin, breathing in the fragrant mountain air Nathan approached from the sawmill. He took her into his arms. "I've just stoked up the boiler, so I have a half hour or so before I can get to work. Is there any coffee left?"

Andriette led him into the cabin and refreshed his cup. They sat at the table, both smiling. "I had such fun yesterday. I always enjoyed Fourth of July Celebrations in Council Bluffs, but they weren't nearly the fun and silliness of yesterday in Dillon."

"I enjoyed the ball game." Nathan replied. "Those miners really knew what they were doing. There were so many home runs and good plays."

"I thought the prospectors did a good job of fielding the baseball, they just couldn't hit the ball as hard as the miners. The miners just have such strong arms and shoulders that they were unstoppable."

"The games after the baseball game were fun, too." Nathan said, rubbing his shoulder.

" You did a super job yourself, throwing a baseball at the target booth, and I thought I'd die laughing watching rough and burly miners try to run in that three-legged race." They both giggled.

"I was really impressed by the drilling races."

Andriette quickly added, "I had no idea what hard work it is to drill into the ground for mining."

"The teams that competed were tremendous. The demonstration of double jacking was simply amazing." They both sat remembering the way one man held the steel bit to the rock while the other man swung the eight pound sledge hammer. After every hit, the bit man turned the bit and helped it bite farther and farther into the rock. "I'm sure that you'd have to be strong to swing that hammer so hard and so fast." Andriette observed.

"True," answered Nathan, "but think of how much trust and courage you'd have if you were the man holding that bit. You'd have to hold it still with all that power from the hammer aimed right at your hands."

Andriette remembered a conversation she'd heard during the picnic. They'd spread a blanket near the first base line to watch the game. Happily, Elizabeth and Keith Janing from the mercantile sat on a blanket next to them. Another woman was on a blanket nearby, watching her husband play for the Miners.

"Did you hear the gossip about Malachi Dillon?" the woman asked Elizabeth.

"I haven't heard anything, is he alright?" Elizabeth replied.

"Well, my niece lives in Goshen County, and her latest letter says that Malachi Dillon was convicted of voluntary manslaughter there in 1892!"

"Not really?" Elizabeth returned. "He is such a nice man. How did he get involved in something that serious?"

"I certainly do not know. But it makes a body wonder if Mr. Dillon has been to prison and is a released convict or if he is a desperate escapee living in Dillon as a respectable man while he really is a fugitive."

The woman, who was clearly enjoying the gossip she was sharing, went on to other topics soon after.

Andriette told Nathan the news she'd heard. Nathan was surprised but not shocked. He had known Dillon for a long time, and knew he was hard driving in everything he tried and a shrewd business man. They talked about it for a while and decided that Malachi Dillon was nothing but honorable and peaceable with them and anyone they knew. Andriette decided that the story was probably just a tale.

The only cloud on a perfect Fourth of July was the sad news that Grant Jones, writer and editor of the *Doublejack*, was dead. Mary Nell told Andriette about it while they walked with Claire through the booths before the picnic and game. "What a shame," Mary Nell was saying, "he was so handsome and such a good writer. What makes a man with so much going for him drink himself to death?"

"Doc Alexander told my husband that Grant was on a drinking binge and then someone at the boarding house in Battle where he was staying gave him some morphine for his bad cough. The morphine and the booze are what killed him."

"Whatever happened, it's a loss to all of us. I loved reading the paper, especially the page he called Grant Jones' Anvil. There were always great stories and poems to read. One minute he'd have you laughing, the next near tears. Often I'd spend the rest of the day thinking about something he'd said."

Andriette reviewed the conversation with Nathan as they sat at the table. "It is such a waste," was Nathan's only comment. He finished his coffee and stood up. At first he looked ready to go out to work, but he stopped and reached out for Andriette's hand. She stood and he took her in his arms and began leading her in a dance.

"My most favorite part of the Independence Day celebration was dancing with you last night."

She smiled and nodded as she let him lead her around the cabin in a waltz. The mine superintendent commissioned some men to build a large dance floor. Several of the miners banded together to form a band for the evening, so Nathan and Andriette and the rest of the town enjoyed an evening dancing under the stars of the Sierra Madres to guitar, fiddle, and harmonica music.

They finished their dance; Nathan kissed her on the forehead, then headed for the saw mill. Andriette tidied up and did the breakfast dishes.

Later, Andriette sat in her meadow with her back resting comfortably against her prayer rock. *Lord, I am so thankful for all the blessings you have provided. Thank you so much for Nathan and his love for me. Thank you for his sweetness and for Daisy, his special gift to me. Lord, there is nothing that I need or want that I don't have, and I thank you for that. Thank you for America, and thank you for the great day yesterday. God, bless Nathan, and keep him safe as he works at the mill and while he delivers the lumber he cuts. Take care of Lillian, Abby and her family, and my father and aunts. God, bless anyone who ever sits in this meadow or by this rock. Give them the peace and security that you give me here. Thank you. Amen.*

She sat a while longer to write in her journal. Eventually, her thoughts turned to the next few months. Nathan and Andriette planned to spend winter at the cabin, so there was much to do.

Chapter 20

August 21, 2007

Hannah spent the evening in the cabin reading. There were many books to choose from in the cabin, but tonight she went to a plain grey box on one shelf. The box was specially made to safely house and preserve the papers within. Hannah tenderly opened the lid and looked at the rag-tag newspapers her father collected through the years. Sometimes he found them at rummage or garage sales where the seller had no appreciation of the history and heritage they possessed. A few he found and purchased on E Bay. Still others were copies of the papers that he and Hannah researched and printed at the State Archives office in Cheyenne. Whether the original or a copy, the papers were precious for their stories and news.

Hannah knew that Grant Jones was the publisher and primary writer for the *Dillon DoubleJack for* the first six months of its existence, then others took over. Jones was a gifted newspaperman who started out as a writer for the *Chicago Times-Herald*. He was known for his coverage of the Republican Convention that nominated William McKinley and was sought after as a dinner speaker. Jones made his way to Colorado and wrote an article for the Rocky Mountain News about the copper strike at Rudefeha. Not long afterward, he moved to Dillon and started the *DoubleJack.* Hannah picked out a paper dated February 7, 1903. She read about an avalanche that roared through the mountains and claimed the lives of two men. The article described the efforts to find the men and recover their bodies. In the section of the paper called "Grant Jones' Anvil" Hannah read carefully, enjoying the language and the spelling as Jones described the events:

> In no other place in the Battle Lake country are the mountains so precipitous as on the south side of Cow creek by Station No. Three. Here the tramway goes over a brink nearly seven hundred feet from the first floor below and over 2,300 feet from the first spot that a tower could be placed to support the steel cables. This is the longest span on the tramway: this is the highest wall of rock in this country, and this is where the snowslide occurred on Jan. 20th! Here a mighty bank of rock extends along the south side of Cow creek canon for more than a third of a mile in almost uninterrupted grandeur, and so precipitous is this masonry in places that to try to scale it would be like trying to climb a perpendicular wall 1,000 feet high.
>
> Above this awful chasm is a bench, or gently sloping mountain side, which in the recent snowslide served as a reservoir for holding thousands of tons of snow, at the very brink of an eternity below.
>
> And so strange is nature, and so equally balanced are her works, that this immense reservoir of snow paused at that very brink, when a stone cast from a child's hand might have jarred it from its holdings and sent it thundering below!
>
> Upon this bench of snow, Peter LeMieux and C. G. Comer, the linemen, tread carelessly with their light web shoes on January 20th, and quick as thought, the mountain side began to move, and then to fly – and they were lost in a Niagra of snow and trees and rocks, and were landed lifeless in the pit below!
>
> It was Death's trap, and they touched the trigger! An ocean of snow rushed sardonically around them and their shroud was snow!

Hannah continued reading the accounts of the men who came from Battle and Dillon and Encampment to find the missing men after their wives became concerned. She reflected on how hard life was back then. The events were sad, but the writing conjured heroes and courage, and because of this, it was uplifting instead of morbid.

Hannah returned to the paper and read one final item, a poem by Grant Jones entitled

"The Snowslide"

In the sky a snowflake once was dropped
by angel children at their play.
Through ethereal air it floated down,
and high upon a mountain top,
It hid within the petals of a columbine.
A poet, loitering by, had watched the
jewel in its fall, and breathless ran
to take it from the flower.
But lo! The snowflake sparked once, and
vanished from his sight; while its
moist kiss was still upon the flower.
The poet trembling stood, and wondered
long, why a thing so pure and
frail had fallen to earth!

A snowflake on Bridger Peak is a
perfect symbol of purity.
A snowslide on Bridger Peak is an
awful instrument of destruction.
The one is as beautiful and frail
as anything on earth.
The other is as mighty and terrible
as any phenomenon of nature.

Hannah finished reading the newspaper and returned it to the archive box. She heated water and made herself some tea. She let herself get lost in the thought of how fragile and unpredictable life can be.

Chapter 21

August 8, 1903

"Nathan," Andriette began this conversation at the end of breakfast. "I've been thinking about winter coming. The dirt floor in the cabin is hard packed and works really well for us in the summer, but I'm thinking it will be icy cold with the winter."

"That's true, it does get cold."

"I was wondering if we might be able to afford a large braided rug like this one in the Sears Catalog." She reached for the book on the hutch. The book itself was orange and black with "Sears Roebuck and Co. Cheapest Supply House on Earth" written on the front. Both Nathan and Andriette enjoyed reading each page, looking at products from guns to tonics, from gramophones to buggies. She opened it to a page she'd marked. "I know it is expensive, but this rug would be big enough to cover nearly all the floor of the cabin."

Nathan looked at it carefully, then got a stern expression. "Andriette, I can't be spending our hard-earned money on frivolous things right now. You're just going to have to wear four pairs of socks and get tough."

Andriette saw the teasing in his eyes and got a scowl to match his. "Certainly, Sir."

He leaned over and kissed her forehead. "I think that's a great idea. Get the order ready today. I expect Walt this morning, and he can take the letter to be mailed. I think you do need to order some socks, too, though."

"That's not all of my idea."

"Really? How much is the next part going to cost?" she knew he was teasing her.

"My grandmother from South Dakota used to talk about living in a sod dugout cabin when she was small. They used to put a layer of straw on the floor, then put a rug on top. She talked about how warm the house was with that added insulation."

"That's really a terrific idea." Nathan answered. "I'll ask Walt to pick up a few bales of straw when he next goes to Encampment."

In the next few weeks, Nathan also ordered some plaster, then showed Andriette how to apply a bit of it between the logs of the cabin to make it more airtight. She worked hard inside and outside the cabin to add a layer to the existing chinking.

One afternoon when Nathan returned to the cabin, Andriette met him at the door. Her face was flushed and her hair messy. "You look like you've been working hard this afternoon. What are you up to?"

"Nathan, if you think it is silly, I'll change it, but I read a book about medieval castles once, and they put tapestries on the walls for warmth. Tell me what you think."

She stepped back and motioned for him to enter the cabin. The cabin looked different from when he'd first brought her here. The rug and straw on the floor gave their house a homey, welcoming feel already. What Andriette did also added to the coziness.

"Not only will that quilt on the wall by our bed make it warmer in here, Andri, but it looks really nice like that."

"Do you really think so?"

He turned and hugged her, nuzzling her neck. "It's wonderful, and you're wonderful," he answered. "In fact, I think maybe we could hang another one along this front wall, too."

"Great idea, but I don't have any more quilts that we don't need on the bed," she answered.

"How about this?" He pulled away far enough to look at her. "We need to stock up on supplies for the winter, and you haven't been to Encampment for a long while. Let's leave in the morning and go. I know that Mother has quilts in an old trunk that I'm sure she'd love for you to use. We'll go visit for a few days and get stocked up for winter."

Andriette didn't try to curb her excitement. A trip to Lillian's and in to town was always a treat.

She packed her old satchel with a few things for the trip, placing the July 4, 1903 *Dillon DoubleJack* safely on the top. Nathan noticed what she was doing and asked about it.

"I want to take this article to show your mom, I want to make sure she saw it, it's so clever."

The trip to Encampment was like a vacation for Nathan and Andriette and also for Lillian. Abby and Mark and toddler Harrison joined them for dinner the second night they were there. Harrison was playing in the yard as the adults finished their coffee on the front porch. There was a good view of the sunset and the mountains along with a clear view of the tram coming in from the mine. They spoke for a few minutes about the ever-present sound of pulleys and cables, then sat quietly enjoying the evening. Andriette asked if Lillian had seen the *DoubleJack*. When Lillian admitted she hadn't, Andriette showed her an article on the first page.

"Andriette, would you read it out loud for us, I am sure all of us will enjoy it," Lillian asked.

"I'd like that," she answered and began reading the article:

> Battle, Wyo. July 1. Colonel A.A. McCoy, an old time Indian fighter of Battle, had a terrible experience last week while fishing on Battle Lake. The colonel was standing on the shore quietly fishing for trout when an awful snorting noise that resounded through the hills attracted his attention. Turning his eyes to the center of

> the lake, he saw a horrible monster. Its hideous head was turned towards him and was elevated about ten feet out of the water. The head seemed long and flat almost like that of an immense whale. A great horn of bone or ivory projected from the nose. The eyes protruded from the head, and its fierce whisker like appendages stuck straight out. The monster's body was covered with heavy, bony scales and its enormous serrated tale lashed the water into a foam. From head to tail the monster measured about fifty feet and its body was of an average thickness of about four feet.
>
> The colonel stood spellbound while the animal, snorting constantly, moved with great rapidity toward the shore where a horse was grazing. With a terrible start it plunged its great horn into the horse's body and thus impaled bore him back into the water and disappeared beneath its surface. The wild commotion caused by the loud snorting and the lashing up of the water seemed to terrify the birds in the trees and caused them to chatter loudly in the fear while the fish sought to lower depths.
>
> Battle Lake, the scene of the affair, is a beautiful little body of water in the mountains near the town of Battle and about seven miles from Dillon. It is clear and cool, reaching great depth in places and abounds in trout. No one in the district has ever seen the animal before but an Indian legend of a monster, Ong Pawkee (bony monster), living near this lake seems to be based upon it. The monster is apparently amphibious and is supposed to live in a cave near the lake, Battle Lake is already famed as the scene of a bloody engagement between Jim Baker and the Indians in early days and from which the name is derived."

The family laughed at the creative article. "I will certainly miss articles like this now that Grant Jones is gone," Lillian said. "I have enjoyed his Cogly Woo and One-Eyed Screaming Emu stories."

Abby agreed and then added, "He was very clever, but could write beautifully as well. I was really touched by his sensitivity and eloquence when the avalanche happened in December."

"I am glad that George Reker is taking the paper over," Nathan remarked. "I'd hate to lose the news we get every week from it."

***

Nathan and Andriette enjoyed several visits like this to Encampment, but also treasured living year-round in their cabin on Haggarty Creek for the next four years. Summers were filled with hard work and busy days. Winters were slower, by November, the snow was deep enough to make travel, even to Dillon, nearly impossible. Blizzards roared through the mountains, the snow and wind howled around the cabin. During those days, Andriette spent quiet days sewing and cooking and praying. Nathan tended to get more restless. Early the first winter, he attached a rope, about waist high, to the edge of the cabin by the door with the other end firmly attached to the barn. Using this, he could safely make his way, even in blinding and deep snow, from the cabin to the barn. He made the trip between the two buildings two or three times a day in bad weather, to check on the horses and work on the upkeep of the wagon and other essentials of the saw mill. Evenings would find him by the fire, next to Andriette in the cabin, mending harnesses or planning for the summer. During blizzards, they created a tradition of cuddling up in a blanket and rereading their letters from the carved box. They took turns reading the letters out loud.

"When I received each letter, I read it a thousand times. I imagined the sound of your voice." Andriette told Nathan. "You were in my heart before we ever met."

"Every letter I wrote took me a week or better to finish. I was sure you'd think I was ignorant. I agonized over spelling. I didn't have a dictionary, and my spelling is pretty bad. I don't know how you made sense of these." Nathan shrugged and smiled.

To fight cabin fever they spent as much time outdoors as they could. They enjoyed trips out into the woods on the skis Andriette rummaged from Lillian's attic. As often as they could, when the weather broke for a day or two, they treated themselves to a trip to Dillon. Sometimes they travelled on foot, with snowshoes Nathan bought for them as a Christmas present the first year they were in the mountains. Other times, they'd ride the horses up.

Their lives settled into a contented routine no matter what the weather was outside. The long days of winter gave them opportunity to talk and reflect and plan. Their love for one another grew, as did their trust and respect. Nathan learned he could share his plans and worries with his wife and trust that she would make helpful insights and suggestions.

***

Spring arrived in the mountains in May, 1907. The air was still crisp in the morning, and nights were still cold, but the sun warmed the air during the day. The snow began to melt, and Haggarty Creek was swollen with run-off. Green shoots of grass and the purple heads of mountain crocuses appeared overnight through the snow. Andriette was able for the first time in several weeks to make her way to the meadow. The ground was too wet to sit by her rock, so she stood leaning against it and marveled at the speed with which spring changed the earth. She was happy and content. It was a balm to her heart to be back in the meadow. The only dark cloud to touch her that day was that they had not yet conceived a child. Andriette knew that Nathan wanted very much to have children, and she did, too. She hoped that she would start this spring knowing she was carrying a baby, and was disappointed that she wasn't. She spent some time in prayer that morning on that issue. *Lord, I want to be a mother, and I think Nathan would be a good father. You know what you have planned for us. Thy will be done.* She stayed for a time in the meadow, just absorbing the sunshine and listening to the world waking up after its winter sleep. The birds were returning and were noisy in their plans for nesting and living the summer in the mountains. Squirrels quarreled with each other in the trees overhead. It was a great day with promise for all that was to come, and Andriette left the meadow with peace and faith that all was as it should be.

Chapter 22

August 21, 2007

A line of boxes crowded the back of the Encampment Grocery Store. Business was light this afternoon and Bob Warren listened to country music and refilled shelves. His wife, Carrie, was sitting behind the register working on the books. He decided he needed a refill of his coffee when he saw Harvey Layton park his green Forest Service truck out front.

"Howdy, Harvey,"

"How's it going?"

"I was just refilling my coffee, want some?"

"It smells great, yes, please."

Bob got a clean mug from the back, filled it and handed it to Harvey.

"You look tired, Harv. Rough night?"

"Nothing too bad. There was some vandalism at one of the sites over at Jack Creek Campground yesterday. I got home late from dealing with that. Then I got woke up early this morning by a phone call from the sheriff in Baggs. Didn't get enough beauty sleep."

"What's up with the sheriff?"

"Some fella walked away from a prison work camp near

Rawlins last week. They think he could be somewhere around here."

They talked for a few minutes more about the news, then the conversation turned to the weather and fishing. Harvey and Bob were both fly fishermen who enjoyed spending time out on the Encampment River together.

They were making plans for their next trip when Harvey's radio interrupted them. A static filled voice called for Captain Layton. Harvey shrugged at Bob. He pulled his radio from the holder on his belt and answered the dispatcher's call. Reception inside the building was bad, so Harvey stepped outside to talk. Bob went back to the box he'd been emptying.

A couple minutes later, Harvey came back into the store. He finished his coffee with a quick gulp and sat the mug near the cash register.

"Thanks for the coffee. Time to go to work."

"More problems?"

"Yeah, looks like I get to drive over near Haggarty Gulch to Lost Creek Campground. Some guy in a beat up old truck was hassling campers there."

Bob watched as Harvey left the store and got into his truck.

Chapter 23

August 21, 1907

Andriette could hear the buzzing of the saw down the hill. She thought about her trip to Dillon two days before. She'd enjoyed playing with Claire's newest son, born healthy in March. She and Claire drank tea and caught each other up on the latest news.

They received a long letter from Lillian. All was well in Encampment, the smelter was busy and everyone was enjoying the high price of copper, $26 per pound. The tram carried ore mined by over two hundred miners in Rudefeha. Rambler now was a town with three grocery stores, two hotels and three bars. Copperton's population reached nearly sixty, and Dillon was growing. Even though all appeared to be smooth and stable, there were rumors of trouble at the mine and financial woes as well. The mine was heavily financed and all hinged on the price of copper. People in the valley and in the mountains were fearful of what would happen if the price of copper fell.

Andriette tidied up and thought about her conversation with Nathan the night before. He seemed distracted and wasn't very talkative. Andriette patiently waited, knowing when he was in a mood like this he would talk when ready, so she put the meal on the table and ate quietly. He finished most of the food on his plate, then Nathan began to talk.

"Andriette, I know everything seems great right now, but I have a feeling that this won't last. If something happened to the mine, say the copper prices went down for example, it could mean hard times for us."

"Nathan, there are lots of businesses and people moving into the valley who will need lumber besides the mines, won't you be able to find customers there?"

"Probably some, but there are big operations working who are already established in the valley. I'm going to need to make some new connections."

"Could Lillian help you with that through her customers at the store in Encampment?"

"That's a good idea. If we did some advertising at the store and Mother kept an eye out for customers, that would be a help," Nathan answered, thinking.

"What if you took some lumber down to the store and she kept some on hand to sell? I know you usually take orders, but if she had some to sell, people in town may buy some of it for smaller projects."

He smiled then, for the first time that evening. "You have good ideas, Mrs. Jameson, I think I should hire you."

"I'm sorry, Sir, I already have a job I am very happy with."

The atmosphere of the evening lightened then, and the couple took a walk after supper dishes were done. They walked hand in hand through the woods, enjoying the evening quiet and the company.

After dinner, Nathan wrote to Lillian with Andriette's idea. If she liked it, and he knew she would, within the month, Nathan could send a load of lumber down to the store with Walt.

As Andriette finished straightening up the cabin Nathan came in. "I've been thinking about what you said about advertising and working with Mother's store in Encampment. It got me thinking. I know the man in Baggs who runs the hardware store. He's a tough old bird, and not very friendly, but he knows quality when he sees it and he likes to make a profit. I have been thinking about going to Baggs with a nice load of lumber, and asking him if he'd do a trial deal with me to sell lumber."

"That's a terrific idea. If that goes well, then you may want to branch out to stores in Saratoga and even Rawlins."

"That's exactly what I was thinking." He was quiet for a minute. "Andriette, I have a load all ready to go. I think that I will leave in the morning for Baggs. I will meet with Mr. Hardiger and discuss the deal and see if he'll go for it. Will you be alright if I'm gone a couple days?"

"Sure, I've been here by myself before. We have plenty of meat and supplies. You know I feel safe and comfortable here."

"I know, but I still don't like leaving you." He smiled. "I don't like sleeping without you, either."

She just smiled in reply.

The next morning Nathan was up early. He was nervous and excited to get started. "You'll be alright?" He asked her several times.

"Of course! Don't worry about me, just go sell our idea to Mr. Hardiger. Take some time to relax once you see him, and come back tomorrow."

"I plan to be back tomorrow night, but don't worry if I don't make it. It might take more than a day to make the deal, so I might be gone more than one night."

"Nathan, will you quit worrying about me? I will be fine. I have a garden to weed. I have sewing to do. I'll be fine."

Nathan embraced her. They stood a long moment, holding each other. He pulled away just far enough to look at her. "Andriette, I love you. You are the best thing that ever happened to me, and I am thankful to God that you wrote such beautiful letters that captured my heart, and then had the courage to come out here to me. I am a better man because of you."

His words touched her heart. "Nathan, I love you more than you can know. The life we have here is perfect, and you are about to make it even more successful. Go. Good luck. Just be your open and honest self, and you'll make the deal, no matter how much of an old codger Mr. Hardiger is."

He kissed her and got up on the loaded buckboard. "Nathan, I love you."

He tipped his hat and moved the rig down the road. He spent the trip thinking about what he'd say to make the deal happen, and he prayed for God's help. The trip went smoothly, and by one o'clock he was in Baggs. He decided to check into the hotel first so that he could clean up and change clothes. He wanted to make a good impression. He entered Hardiger's hardware store about an hour later.

"Good afternoon," he addressed the lady who was working behind the counter. "I am hoping to talk with Mr. Hardiger."

"You just missed him. He just left with a load of supplies for a ranch outside of town."

"When do you expect him back?"

"Not 'til tomorrow afternoon. Can I help you?"

Nathan was disappointed, but didn't let it show. "No, Ma'am. I will come back tomorrow afternoon. You say he'll be in the store then?"

"I expect so. Can I give him a message?"

"My name is Nathan Jameson, Ma'am."

"I'll tell him."

Nathan was frustrated at the delay, but not concerned. He took the buckboard to the livery and helped the livery agent unhook the horses and settle them in. Then he walked through the main street of Baggs. He was encouraged, there was growth happening here, and that was a good sign. He also noticed that the hardware store was still the only one in town and there was no sign that they already sold lumber.

Nathan slept well that night after a nice supper. He went to sleep praying for the deal and thinking of Andriette.

The next morning, his nervousness was back. The morning went slowly, he checked his pocket watch often, and the time seemed slow. He ate breakfast at a small diner near Hardiger's store, and enjoyed listening to the conversations around him.

Finally, it was after one, and he made his way to the store. When he entered, he was encouraged to see that Mr. Hardiger was back and helping a customer. He waited patiently, at least on the outside, for the man to get free. When he was, Nathan approached him and held out his hand. "Mr. Hardiger, I'm Nathan Jameson. We met a year or so ago when I needed some parts for my buckboard."

"I remember you, Jameson. I hear you were looking for me yesterday. What can I do for you?" His words were polite, but his rough look and gruff voice spoke otherwise. Nathan pitched his idea to the man as a good way to branch out and make more money.

The older man seemed unconvinced but did agree to accompany Nathan to the livery and inspect the load of lumber he brought. Nathan prayed silently as they walked.

Hardiger looked over the load carefully. Nothing in his face or voice gave away what he was thinking.

"Jameson, how reliable are you? Can you keep me supplied with high quality goods?"

"I've been at this for a long time, Mr. Hardiger. I have many satisfied customers in the mountains around here and in Encampment. I guarantee I can meet your demand and fill custom orders as well."

"That's a mighty big promise for a one man operation."

"If the need grows, I won't stay that way for long. As it is, I don't do the logging myself, and I have two men who help with the delivering, so I already have help."

"Jameson, I'm willing to take this on a trial basis. I'll take this load of lumber, and two more just like it. We'll see how it goes from there. If the three loads sell, I'll be willing to discuss a contract with you."

Nathan put out his hand, "Thank you, Sir, I am sure that this will be a good business decision for both of us."

They discussed and agreed on terms then. Nathan was elated that the deal was done and excited because they settled on an amount that he thought was fairly high. Hardiger left him to return to the store. Nathan hitched up the team to the buckboard so that he could deliver the lumber.

Nathan was excited to get home and share with Andriette the great news. He checked his watch, it was three o'clock. If he unloaded and hurried, he could make it home by ten or eleven. He looked at the clouds building on the horizon, threatening rain, and he decided then that he'd stay one more night in Baggs and have a celebratory supper, then start for home early tomorrow. He didn't know that his decision would change everything.

Chapter 24

August 22, 2007

Hannah awoke with a new attitude when morning dawned. She'd slept well in her new room downstairs, and was greeted by a perfect mountain morning. The sky was a hue of deep, infinite blue that appears nowhere else but the high mountains. The breeze was light. The sun warmed the trees around her so that they gave off their fresh pine fragrance. Hannah sat on the front deck with a cup of tea and an apple, watching the hummingbirds squabble at the feeder.

She felt light. She knew that when she returned to work on Monday, she'd still have problems. William Bates still had it out for her, and a letter from her Dad and a few days in the mountains wouldn't fix that. Examining her heart, she realized that where Greg had been was now a tender scar, nearly healed. Dad's words resounded yet again in her mind. *Think carefully about your life, then live it with abandon.* She thought carefully about her relationship with Greg, and the right thing to do was to break it off. Now she was back in control and free to live her life on her own terms, *with abandon*, not trying to be something she wasn't.

Hannah resolved to call her mom when she got a cell signal in Encampment. She knew that her behavior towards her mom was childish, and she wanted dearly to talk to her, to tell her about Dad's letter and apologize for being bratty. Hannah wasn't sure if other people would understand how a letter could make such a difference, but it had. One last time, her dad understood her and showed her he loved her. He'd forgiven her so that she could forgive herself. As the hummingbirds argued and the bright mountain sun warmed her, Hannah considered what he'd said about time. Did the power of a prayer fade like a rainbow or disappear like the dew on the leaves in the morning? Or did prayers last? She couldn't find an answer to this, since the only cloud still lingering on the horizon for Hannah was her relationship with God. She was still ambivalent there. She just hadn't yet come to terms with God's choices lately. Refusing to even think about it, Hannah picked up the book she'd started last night before sleeping. She found it on the shelf, and she'd not seen it before. *To Dance With Kings* by Rosalind Laker, a thick historical novel about the castle of Versailles in France. The opening chapter transported her to France in 1664, and she gladly settled in for a good read.

She read most of the morning, and then decided she needed a walk. She considered as she was coming to terms with the past, she needed to begin to create a present and look at the future. She and Dad had great times here, and she'd have more on her own. *Eventually I will bring someone very special here,* she thought, *and then children of my own.* Time would continue to draw circles in her life.

She refreshed the water in her canteen and grabbed her rucksack. She decided to leave the camera behind. This time she walked out the back door and went northeast. She'd decided to make the east corner her goal, maybe she could see some deer or elk in the valley below. As she walked away from the cabin she heard the noise of a motor in the direction of the highway.

She took her time and let her mind wander. It didn't take her long to find herself on the granite point overlooking the valley. Though she saw no big game, a tiny chipmunk ventured up on the rocks beside her. She laughed at his antics as he retrieved the crumbs from the granola bar she tossed him.

Hannah sat surveying the land before her for a long time. The solitude enfolded her. As the sun began to make its way down into the tops of the trees to her west, Hannah started for the cabin.

The walking was easy, as she approached the cabin she knew there was still plenty of daylight left to make a nice dinner for herself. Her feet on the wooden stairs of the porch were loud in the calmness of the late afternoon. Hannah dropped her rucksack on the chair outside and went into the cabin. It took a few steps in for her eyes to adjust.

He was sitting in the easy chair.

"Hello, Darlin'," his voice was soft.

Hannah's first reaction was anger. This was the man she'd talked to yesterday by the gate. She'd made it clear then that this was private property and he wasn't invited.

"I'd like you to leave," she growled, recrossing the room and opening the front door.

He slowly stood and walked toward her and the door. For a second, Hannah believed he would walk out the door and that would be the end of it. Instead, as he came beside her, he reached out and grabbed her arm. "I told you before I think this looks like a good place to hunt."

"Let go of me!" Hannah tried to jerk her arm free, but his grip tightened.

"Well, look here." His voice was deeper and took on a threatening timbre. "I think I bagged myself a wildcat."

In an instant all of Hannah's anger drained away and pure fear took its place. She was frozen, unable to make a move or a sound.

Still gripping her arm tightly, he reached up with his other hand to push the door closed. Then he gently pushed a strand of hair away from Hannah's face and smiled down at her. "That's right, Darlin', settle down and be easy. You and I are going to have a nice time together, aren't we?"

Slowly, Hannah's brain began to function. "I really think you better go. My husband will be back soon, and he won't like it that you are here."

"Nice try, Babe, but you're alone. You were alone in Encampment, and no one but you has been here."

It was as if he'd slapped her. "You've been watching me?" she squeaked out.

"I'm a hunter you see, and I got you in my sights at that little store. Part of the fun of a hunt is stalking the prey."

A new wave of fear washed over Hannah. She felt sick to her stomach. She tried to figure out a way to get control of the situation, but her panic overwhelmed her.

"You took a nice long walk. I'm betting you're hungry. I am. So let's you and me go make some supper."

His grip on her arm relaxed a little, she could tell that he was testing her to see if she was going to cooperate or fight him. Stunned and numb, Hannah walked complacently with him to the kitchen. He let go of her arm and watched her as she took the steak out of the cooler. He seemed pleased at her actions and smiled at her.

"That's right, we're going to have a nice meal, then we'll have some real fun."

Hannah turned from him then and started the task of stoking up the stove. The physical space between them helped her gain a modicum of control over her terror, and her mind began to whirl with possible options. She forced herself to think. There was no way she could overpower him. He was wearing the same tee shirt and jeans as yesterday, and the muscles under the light fabric of the shirt were clear and well defined.

She walked to the other side of the kitchen and grabbed a couple more small logs to add to the fire box of the stove. As she did so, she noticed a long hunting knife in a leather sheath hung from his belt on his left side. Numbing, blinding panic threatened to overtake her once again.

She got out the potatoes and carrots, glancing again at her captor. He was sitting, loose and relaxed, in the chair closest to the back door. She'd never have time to get out if she tried to escape, he was too close. She willed her hands to stop shaking as she peeled the potatoes and put them and the carrots on the stove to boil. Just as she was finishing, he came up behind her.

He trapped her body by putting his hands on the counter around her and leaning in to her. He kissed and nuzzled her neck. Hannah entertained no doubts about what his plans were. She knew she had to get out of the cabin or else.

Chapter 25

August 22, 1907

Andriette stood and watched as Nathan disappeared down the road. She would miss him, of course, but she was certain that this venture would be good for him so she wasn't worried about being alone. When she couldn't see him or hear the rig anymore, she returned to the cabin. She cleaned up the kitchen and washed the breakfast dishes. She spent some time on other housework. The day was warm, and Andriette weeded the garden, which didn't take her long. She smiled to herself, thinking that this little garden got more attention than it really needed because she enjoyed being out there so much. The potatoes were doing well, and green beans were flowering. Tiny carrot tops, lacy and brave, pushed up in neat rows. She could already picture neat and tidy army of jars filled with green and orange on the cabin shelf. She didn't plan to can all the carrots, though. Some she would pick and store in straw in the barn as well. The variety would be welcome when the snows set in. She smiled as she worked as she added a prayer for the meals they would share over this food and the blessings of their little harvest.

As the afternoon began, Andriette washed her hands and decided to go for a walk. She wanted to spend some time in prayer for Nathan and his meeting in Baggs. She tucked a piece of bread in the pocket of her dress along with a slice of cheese thinking she would treat herself to a small picnic, and started out. As an afterthought, she grabbed her journal and a pencil, too. The walk up to the meadow was refreshing after being bent over in the garden. The wind was blowing the tops of the trees overhead, but because of the thickness of the forest, there was just a refreshing breeze touching her face. She stopped at the edge of the meadow to gather a handful of wild raspberries to add to her picnic, then continued to her rock. She sat down and leaned back against it. Feeling its warmth, she imagined that this was how God hugged her.

She sat for some time without conscious thought. She slowly ate, relishing the thickness of the bread, the hearty sharpness of the cheese and the delight of the raspberries. All was right with her world, and thought wasn't necessary. Being was enough.

Finally, Andriette began to put her thoughts into words. Knowing there was no human around for miles who could hear her and think her crazy, she spoke to God aloud. She poured her heart out to Him, thanking him for the blessings of the day and of her life. She never imagined, in her stifled life in Council Bluffs that it was possible to be this happy or fulfilled. She grew silent after a while and opened her journal. She began with prayer for Nathan: asking Him for wisdom and boldness for Nathan in talking to the man in Baggs, and for safety and leading for what was to come.

"Father, Nathan is a hardworking man, who sometimes can be a little rough around the edges. Lord, smooth off those edges so that he can glorify You more, and keep him near to you every day. Don't let him prosper just for the sake of being prosperous, but for Your sake." Andriette finished her prayer as she normally did when she sat at the rock in the meadow. "Thank you for this beautiful spot. Thank you for creating it, and thank you for sharing it with me. Lord Jesus, I ask you to bless any person who ever comes into this meadow or sits at this rock. Be real to that person draw them near to You. Protect them, and help them to find safety and comfort here and in You."

Andriette sat for a few more minutes, then realized that the sun had dipped below the mountain ridge in the west. On the plains, in Baggs, it would still be afternoon, but at the cabin, deep in the forest and at the bottom of the valley, it was already growing cooler and darker.

She returned to the cabin, noticing that the wind was dying down and the forest was quiet. Off in the distance, Andriette could hear a squirrel chattering, but the forest was otherwise tranquil. She lit the kerosene lamp on the table and rekindled the fire in the stove. She decided that since she was spending the evening and night alone it would be a treat to take a nice bath. That would mean carrying water from the creek, but the extra work would be worth the time to soak in the tub and relax.

The bathtub was an indulgence to her. Most of the time, it sat in one corner of the cabin with a finely sanded piece of wood over the top – making a nice table. Andriette cleared off the top and slid it off, leaning it against the wall behind the tub. She put the plug in the bottom of it, and poured water into the kettle and the pot, putting them both on the stove. She marveled at how Nathan created a drain from the tub to the outside, near her garden, so that while she had to carry water to fill it, she need only pull the plug to empty it, just like at Lillian's. One day they would have running water in the cabin, Nathan told her, but she really didn't mind carrying water. She grabbed two buckets and headed out.

Haggarty Creek was always a good supply of water, but it was a goodly distance from the cabin. What they used for water was a small spring just north and uphill of the barn. Through the first half of the summer, the spring provided plenty of water. It didn't matter where they went along its banks, it was easy to fill up the buckets. In the fall, though, the supply dwindled. Nathan solved the problem the first fall she was here by creating a small pool where the natural course of the spring turned a bit to make its way down the hill to meet the Haggarty. To create the pool, he dug out the bottom, then lined it and the banks around it with rocks. This created a nice, deep depression for the water to well up but that wasn't ever silty or muddy. Andriette was careful for fear of twisting an ankle as she crossed the rocks to the pool.

Wanting to have a good soak, Andriette made two trips for water. On the first trip back to the cabin, she noticed that several of the rocks above the rim of the depression were a bit unstable, probably due to the rain that fell yesterday, and she told herself to be careful where she stepped. It was getting to be twilight when she arrived for her second trip. She filled both buckets and turned to leave the pool. As she did, she sloshed the water in the bucket in her right hand, and got her shoe and leg all wet. She took another step, still a bit off balance, and the small stones underneath her foot rolled. She lost her balance and went down on one knee, hard. The bucket in her left hand upended as she tried to catch herself, and the bottom of the bucket caught one of the large rocks at the rim. Andriette fell to both knees then, wet and crabby with herself at her clumsiness. She took a breath and started to rise when two of the large rocks along the rim gave way and came crashing and rolling down on her. It happened suddenly, there was no time to try to dodge them, as the wet material of her skirt stuck to her legs and made it impossible for her to move quickly. The rocks rolled right over her left foot and ankle, and came to a stop. She was pinned at the bottom of the depression at the very edge of the pool.

Frustration and anger were her first emotions. She found herself in a strange position, most of her weight was on her right hip and she was able to prop herself up a short way using her elbow. Her right leg, though, was pinned under her by her left thigh and the weight of the material of her dress. The rocks that held her were about two feet in diameter. They rested with one on her shin bone and one against the knee of her left leg. Andriette tried using her arms to merely push the rocks off of her, and was surprised to find that she couldn't make them budge. She was in a position that afforded her no leverage, the rocks were heavy and wedged together, and she needed to push them up an incline in order to get them away from her.

Andriette's frustration and anger turned into fury and then desperation as she struggled against the weight and the strange position she was locked into. She tried to push the rocks, she even tried pulling them to at least get them to move. Nothing worked. She looked around for a branch or anything else she could use as a pry bar, but nothing was within her reach. She began to tire, and as she did, she began to feel two new things: pain and cold. She was wet from her waist down due to the spilled water and now being on the damp ground near the spring. The air was cool, and she began to feel cold seeping into her.

Andriette exhausted herself trying to get free. She stopped struggling and was still, sure that it would not be possible for her to move the rocks on her own. Now she registered the pain she was feeling. She recognized that bones in her leg were most surely broken and smashed. What started as a throb quickly grew into a thick blanket of pain from her hip down. From the position she was in, and because her legs were covered by her skirt, she couldn't see that the rocks had also opened a sizable gash in her left calf. Thanks to the cold, she felt the gash only as a deep throb. After a time, the hem of her skirt began to flower with a bright red stain of blood while she bled freely into the ground beneath her. Even though she was spared the complete knowledge of her situation, fear set in. Andriette's heart began to race, and her breathing turned to sobs. She railed against her helplessness. She cried for a few minutes and then regained control. Wiping her eyes, she fished her handkerchief from her pocket, and took a determined breath. Over the rim of rocks that surrounded her she could see the welcoming light of the kerosene lamp through the window of the cabin, so warm and inviting yet so impossibly far away. She made herself think rationally. *Yes, this is going to be a rough night.* She told herself. *I am going to get cold and be uncomfortable, but neither of those will kill me. I have water right here to drink, and I ate not long ago. Nathan will be home tomorrow afternoon, and then all will be well. Lord, I need a bit of help here.*

Her mind began to slow down and she began to hear the night sounds around her. The birds were quiet, crickets chirped. The wind came up in crisp breaths that chilled her. She pulled as much of her skirt as was free around her shoulders. The cloth was damp and didn't provide much warmth, but it did insulate her against the night air. Andriette spent the first part of the night praying and trying to relax and sleep. She did sleep a bit, but the shock and the cold and the incessant throb of the gash on her calf and the heavy pain in her legs kept her from any kind of comfort. She shivered and cried, and tried to hang on. After a while, time stopped mattering. She was aware of movement in the underbrush just a few feet from her. Once she heard something rooting around and pawing the grass just at the tree line. She became fearful then, jumping and starting at the night sounds nearby. She watched and listened, her heart pounding in the dark, hoping that the coyotes and badgers and all the other creatures of the night had other places to be than within distance of her scent.

She was aware enough of herself that when the eastern sky began to lighten and turn pink with the sunrise, she turned hopeful. She felt confident that Nathan would be home soon, and reminded herself of that fact often. With the sun came relief from the cold. The day was beautiful and sunny. She got little actual sunshine where she sat, but the air warmed and she became much more comfortable. The pain in her leg was dull and constant, but she tried to concentrate on thoughts that took her away from herself. She pictured herself sitting in the meadow, relived the moments with the lioness and her cubs, and relayed scenes of working with Nathan at the mill. She began to feel hungry, but reminded herself that she needed to count her blessings and focused on happy times.

She continued to try to free herself. She tried digging with her fingers to create a gap underneath her leg. The rocks merely settled more heavily into her flesh. She began to grow weak with her efforts.

The day wore on. She tried to picture what Nathan was doing at the exact moment, and prayed that he was on his way home. She expected him sometime late afternoon, so when the sun passed overhead and she guessed it to be after three o'clock, she let herself begin to hope he would come soon. As the afternoon wore on, she strained to hear the horses hooves on the forest floor. She imagined once that she heard Nathan's voice calling her.

"I'm here!" she screamed. "Nathan, I'm here, please help me!" She called out for him over and over, then realized in bitter disappointment that what she heard was not him after all.

Night began to fall, and Andriette struggled. She was tired and hungry. After dark, she finally gave in to bitter disappointment that Nathan wasn't returning. The pain in her leg increased. In addition, the rest of her body was miserable from being locked in the same position for now twenty-four hours. Her hips ached. She could lay back and give her right hip some relief for a time, but that exposed her to the dampness of the ground, and she got colder. Around midnight, it began to rain. Andriette was soaked to the skin, shivering uncontrollably. She slept fitfully for a while, and then as the cold and damp seeped farther into her, she slipped quietly into unconsciousness.

Chapter 26

August 22, 2007

Scrambling to keep her thoughts focused on how to handle this situation, Hannah continued to make dinner. She'd considered trying to bash him with the cast iron frying pan, but didn't think she was capable of violence strong enough to stop him, he was big and fit. She knew that her only hope was escape. But how could she get out of the cabin and give herself enough lead time to get away?

Her keys were on the table by the front door, but she doubted she'd have enough time to get to the car, get in it, get it started and drive away. Then there was the shut gate she'd have to deal with. She dismissed the car as a possibility.

As she set the table and drained the potatoes and carrots, he walked around the cabin. He seemed antsy and anxious. He walked from the window to the door several times, and was continually moving his hands. As much to calm herself as him, Hannah began a conversation. "I don't know your name."

"Huh? Yeah, name's Travis." He picked up a frame. In it was a picture of Hannah and her Dad at Battle Lake. "Looks like you and your Daddy had a real close relationship."

"He was a great guy, he taught me how to catch a fish that day," Hannah murmured. She thought about that day at the lake. They'd talked about sea serpents and Thomas Edison. Her

Dad's voice rumbled through her mind, "Girl, you never know what you can do until you do it. And I'm sure you can do anything you decide you want to do, as long as you ask God's help."

As she was thinking, Travis walked up close to her again, he took her arm and pulled her to him. His voice was low, "I'm going to teach you things your Daddy never taught you."

Panic exploded through Hannah, but she kept her mouth closed and her body still. "I need to get the steak before it burns," she stepped away from him. "Go sit down and I'll put the food on."

Hannah put the food on the table. All the time, Travis watched her intently. She sat down, and his eyes left her, falling instead on the meal in front of him. He picked up his knife and fork and started to eat. She sat and watched him a moment and then said, "I'm sorry, but I really need to go to the bathroom. Do you mind if I excuse myself for a minute?" She tried to smile.

"You think I'd just let you walk outside and disappear?" His voice was loud and sharp. His body was instantly tense, his face angry.

"No!" She widened her eyes and tried to calm him down. "There's a porta-potty in my bedroom. I hate going outside." She tried to chuckle, but it came out as almost a cough as she looked at him. "It's just through there." She pointed at the door across the kitchen.

He looked at his plate, and relaxed a little. She could tell he was hungry, and was gauging how much he believed her with how good that steak tasted. "Go on then, but leave the door open a bit. Don't try nothin'."

She let him see the relief on her face and smiled a little, "Thanks," she said, and got up as nonchalantly as she could.

She closed the door about half way and opened the cupboard. She slid the potty out, putting it against the door. It wasn't much, but it would impede him a little. Then, she took a deep breath and exhaled while she prayed. *God, I need your help.*

Hannah didn't hesitate again. She grabbed the sweatshirt that was lying on her bed and, as quietly as she could, she stepped across the room to the open window. In an instant she was through it and running full tilt towards the north. She didn't think about where she was going, only concentrating on putting as much distance between herself and her captor as possible. She had barely begun running when she heard a shout and then the back door slamming. She looked around to see him coming off the porch, moving fast.

She didn't look behind her again. Adrenaline surged through her and she ran for her life. Telling herself that she held the advantage because she knew this area so well, she headed into the heavy timber around Haggarty Creek. Looking around her, she decided to stay in the creek for a little while, heading north east. If he really was a hunter as he'd told her, he might have the skill to track her, but she didn't want to make anything easy for him. She kept low and in the middle of the creek for about a hundred yards, then came out on the other side where she could step on a fallen log and walk on it away from the muddy bank. The noise from the creek disguised all other noises, so she had no idea where he was. If she stayed quiet now, he'd not know where she was either.

Climbing up the side hill, Hannah realized she was very near the old cabin. Her breaths came in gasps, and she knew she needed to stop, but her fear pushed her on. She caught a glimpse of the old boiler off to her right. Continuing on, the meadow was soon ahead of her. She didn't want to let herself be in such an exposed place, so she skirted the meadow and found herself by the big rock. The fear, the run and her exertion at this altitude worked together to bring her to near exhaustion, so she sat down in the shadow of the rock to rest.

Every cell in her brain was saturated with fear. Her body was tense, almost electrified with the need to move. Terror permeated her being, but instead of blind panic, her head cleared and she began thinking with clarity and purpose. She was on her own, with no one within distance to help. She stood at a dangerous brink and she couldn't see what was going to happen next. Will he catch me? Will I be raped or beaten? Will I die? Not knowing and not having control gripped her and wrenched her into a new level of fear. Before her recent troubles began, Hannah always felt in control. She knew what would happen next. When she was living at home, she *knew* she'd go to college. In college she *knew* she'd do well and graduate well and then find a job. She believed that she *knew* what lay in wait for her. Hannah became aware with new eyes that she didn't know what was to come. In the bleakness, Hannah was stunned with an exquisite moment of clarity.

I do not know what is going to happen, nor have I ever.

Hannah always lived thinking she was somehow in charge of her life, or at least able to foresee and manipulate the events of her life. Crouching here, in the shadow of a rock, miles from help, Hannah reviewed her life in one giant snapshot of understanding. She was not now, nor had she ever been, in control of the events of her life. The fact that she couldn't control her father's cancer and his decisions about it, the fact that she couldn't control Greg and his desires for her, the fact that she couldn't control and fix the problems she was having at work. All of these events had been trials for her and difficult to deal with because she was under the false assumption that she could *and should* be controlling the outcomes. In the face of these problems she felt she wasn't making the right choices well enough to make everything turn out right and *therefore she was a failure*.

You aren't a failure because you never were in control. The truth of this thought was so powerful that she forgot for a time about the danger around her. Instead, she concentrated on feeling the amazing lightness within herself. The weight and responsibility for making everything be fine was gone. She experienced a giddy freedom from failure. What replaced it was a secure knowledge that whatever happened was in Someone Else's hands and that she needed to trust.

Incongruously, though she was being hunted, there was finally peace.

"Thank you, Father God."

Hannah said the words aloud, for the rocks and trees to hear. For the past three months, she'd been thinking and longing for her dad, ignoring her Father in heaven. Now, she thankfully grasped that God had provided her with a great dad, in part at least to enable her to connect with and understand Him.

"I get it." She said this aloud as well, then asked for God's forgiveness for her estrangement to Him. Hannah felt herself relax, she felt healed and renewed. Her breathing returned to normal. She started to tune in to the noises around her, to try to pinpoint where her pursuer was. She could hear nothing out of the ordinary.

The sun dipped below the tops of the trees and shadows lengthened. There was still an hour or so before complete dark, and she knew it was essential that she get somewhere safe and secure before then. The timber was just too dense with deadfall to be able to move in the dark.

She sat for a few minutes longer, gaining her strength and forming a plan. Then, her ears picked up a chilling sound. Crouching low, she peaked around the edge of the boulder into the meadow. Travis was on the other side, head down and walking slowly.

It was apparent from his steady, methodical movements that he was tracking her. Again, she prayed silently, "Father God, I am in real trouble here, and I need your help. Show me how to get away."

A memory of her father popped into Hannah's thoughts. Twelve year old Hannah sat at the dinner table with her mom and dad. They discussed a tragic school shooting in the news. Mom handed the butter to Dad and remarked, "I just hope that if I were in a desperate situation, in some sort of horrible danger, that I could keep my head and not just get hysterical."

Dad answered her with assurance, "Philippians 4:13: "I can do everything through him who gives me strength." is what I hope comes to my mind if I ever face danger."

Hannah smiled at the memory and at the wisdom. She slipped her sweatshirt on and quietly moved away from the rock into the timber. She made a plan as she moved. Heading east from here would take her into rough, rocky forest. The rocks would make it harder for him to track her. If she could make it to the east corner of her land, then she could intersect with the Haggarty Gulch road to Dillon. The shepherd's wagon was sitting about a mile up the road from where she hoped she'd come out. If she could make the road, then even in the dark, she should be able to follow it and get help from the shepherd.

It wasn't much of a plan, but it was something. Hannah moved as quickly as she could without running. She tried to step softly and make as little noise as possible. She knew there was nothing she could do to hide her tracks, so she let that worry go.

Every so often she'd stop to listen. Sometimes she'd hear the crack of a branch and know that he was still somewhere behind her. She started down a steep grade, the shadows lengthening and the dark descending. The granite was loose here, and her foot slipped, sending her down on one knee. She used her hand to catch herself and scraped the skin off her palm. In the dimness, she heard a voice through the trees. "Hannah. I am going to find you. I'm coming."

Instantly she was shivering. He was a distance away, she could tell that, but the confidence and sport in his voice chilled her as nothing else had. He was enjoying this!

Despair crowded into her mind, and Hannah began repeating "I can do everything through Him who gives me strength" silently to herself as she walked. She stopped at the bottom of the draw to get her bearings and decide where to go next. She glanced back. A light at the top of the hill she'd just come down bobbed through the trees. He held a flashlight!

Determined not to panic, Hannah took a deep breath, searching her mind for a new verse to help her. "If God is for us, who can be against us," came to her in the dark. *I've been such a brat to you, God*, Hannah prayed, *I trust in your forgiveness and grace, and I trust that You are for me!*

Hannah followed the draw along the hillside. She'd walked for two or three minutes when she heard his voice again. It was much closer this time, taunting and joking through the growing darkness. "Are you getting tired? You might as well just sit down and rest, I'll be right there!"

Fear and anger welled up in Hannah and threatened to overcome her. She knew that she'd never make it to the sheepherder's camp. She darted into some dense trees, scratching her cheek on the way through. She stopped to pray. She was exhausted and coming to the end of her will and her strength. She was sinking into defeat. Looking around her, she realized that she knew where she was. Knowing gave her confidence and anxiety at the same time. She was near where the mountain lion lived, and that certainly added new danger for her, but she was closer to the road and the sheepherder's camp than she expected.

Just as she was feeling encouraged, Travis' voice echoed through the trees. He was much closer now. Very close. "Hannah. I'll be with you in a minute. Don't worry, I'll take good care of you." He laughed then. Tears rolled down her cheeks. She was defeated.

"I will lift up my eyes unto the hills, where does my help come from?" Hannah heard the words in her mind and looked up the hill beside her. Not more than twenty yards above her was the entrance to the cave she and her father explored once. She pictured the inside of it. The entrance was nearly hidden. Its opening was small and dropped off about three feet just inside. Hannah took off as silently as possible. While scrambling up, her feet slipped as granite shards rolled beneath them. She caught herself as her raw, bleeding hand closed around a softball sized rock. She held on to it as she stood up and made her way to the cave opening. She didn't think about the spiders or bugs that would be inside. She didn't stop to consider how claustrophobic a cave in the dark would be. At the cave opening she sat down and put her feet in. Then she edged off into the blackness. Her feet skidded a little as they hit the cave floor. She hesitated only a second, then pushed herself into a small nook to the right of the entrance. She was breathing fast, gulping at the air in her fear of the darkness as well as of Travis. She closed her eyes and concentrated on being calm.

Hannah took stock of her plight. She could hear Travis outside. His steps were loud in the growing twilight. She took a breath to steel herself for the coming moments. With any luck, Travis would not be able to see the opening in the shadows and would pass by her. She held on to the hope that he wouldn't find her. She was surprised to find that she was still gripping the rock she'd picked up when she'd slipped. Forming a second plan, she pictured bashing him if he put his head in to the cave opening. The air in the cave was musty and there was a strong odor she couldn't place. She knew, from when she and Dad explored this cave, that it wasn't very large, and that the short corridor she was tucked into opened to a cavern about four feet wide by twelve feet long. Hannah tried to picture the inside of the cave as she focused on listening to the sounds of Travis' footsteps outside.

A movement behind her sent a shiver through Hannah. What she heard then raised every hair on the back of her neck. It was a low growl, threatening and powerful. She was not alone in the cave.

Chapter 27

August 22, 1907

Nathan's heart was light. He was anxious to share his good news with Andriette, so he started for home early. He bought a couple slices of bread and some coffee from the lady at the cafe and ate them as he left Baggs. He pictured himself telling Andriette about the lucrative deal they'd made and watching the pride and excitement in her eyes. He pulled the wagon to the front of the cabin just as the sun was overhead. He poked his head inside to see if she was there. He checked the garden and then, thinking he knew for certain where she was, he headed up to the meadow. She wasn't there.

Nathan headed back down to the cabin, checking to see if her horse was there, thinking perhaps she went into Dillon for some reason. The horse was there and without hay.

He checked the cabin again, and this time noticed the pots on the stove which were boiled dry and the partially filled bathtub uncovered in the corner. Fear rose in him as he ran toward the spring. What he saw there was his worst nightmare. She was lying by the pool, crumpled and strangely positioned. He thought she was dead. She was so still and ghostly white. He knelt by her side and touched her cheek, it was cold. His fear took hold. He cried out to God. He grabbed each of the two rocks that pinned her and sent them sailing across to the other side of the spring. He gathered her up into his arms and started for the house, still believing that Andriette was dead. As he got to the top rim of the spring, a small movement of her eyelids stopped him. He gently laid her back down and watched her. She stirred a little and whispered, "Nathan, help me."

He kissed her gently then, and assured her over and over that he was there and she was safe as he lifted her again and carried her to the cabin. He hated how cold she felt, so he got her sodden clothes off her. Her skirt, he found, was wet from the rain and water at the pool, but was also soaked and dripping with Andriette's blood. Throwing her clothes in a heap, he saw that her leg was misshapen and clearly broken, and he found the gash on her calf. He bound the wound tightly, but before he was finished, the bandage was already stained with blood. He knew that the movement should be causing her pain, but she only whimpered. He then tried to position her leg so that it looked a bit straighter, watching her face as he moved it. She was gritting her teeth and in great pain. Finally, he wrapped her up in the quilt she and Lillian sewed.

"Nathan, I'm so cold," she whispered.

He covered her with another quilt and got a fire going in the stove. "She needs something warm to drink," he thought as he reached for the tea kettle and realized that there was no water in the cabin. Cursing, he ran to the spring and filled the buckets that Andriette had dropped.

His hands were shaking when he filled the tea kettle and set it on the stove. "God, please." He repeated his prayer over and over.

Nathan knew she needed a doctor, soon. Her leg was badly broken and the cut needed attending. There wasn't a doctor in Dillon, though. The nearest doctor's offices were in Baggs or Encampment. He couldn't leave her that long, and she was in bad shape to make the trip, even in the back of the buckboard.

She seemed to be waking up a bit, and he tried to get her to drink some tea. She did drink a bit, and opened her eyes to look at him.

"Andri, I am so sorry! How long were you down at the spring?"

"I wanted a bath the night you left," she answered weakly, whispering.

Nathan was horrified. She was hurting and in trouble while he treated himself to dinner and a relaxing evening in Baggs. She had been in pain while he indulged himself.

No matter what he did, Nathan could not get Andriette warm. He stoked up the stove and wrapped her up, but she remained cold to the touch. Even though her leg was swollen and misshapen, and certainly caused her pain, the only complaint she made was how cold she felt.

As the afternoon moved sullenly on, Nathan moved as silently as possible in and around the cabin. He brought in wood for the stove and made another quick trip to the spring for water. Each time he saw the spot at the spring where he'd found Andriette and the crimson stained rocks, his fear was renewed as was his disgust with himself for staying in Baggs.

Nathan reckoned it was about four o'clock. There was plenty of wood and water for the night, and stew warmed on a back burner. Nathan made more tea and helped Andriette drink it, and then began to get ready to make a run to Rudefeha. He could fetch Jerry Peterson, who knew a little doctoring and took care of injuries at the mine. Andriette dozed between sips of tea, but she woke up enough to notice his preparations and asked him about them. She could see the shadows of late afternoon through the windows.

"I need to get help, Andri. I will only be gone an hour or two."

Andriette started to panic. "No, Nathan, I am afraid. I don't want to die alone."

Nathan went to her; tears welled up in his eyes as he lay beside her on the bed, cradling her in his arms as best he could while not disturbing the blankets she was wrapped in or moving her leg. "Andri, you aren't going to die," he whispered. His words were to comfort her, and they were a comfort to him as well, yet even as he said them, he knew that there was a strong possibility that Andriette would not survive. She had been cold and wet for so long and lost so much blood.

Andriette's voice was weak, but her words were strong. "Nathan, I truly think I won't make it through tonight."

Nathan began to argue, but she put her finger on his lips. He stopped, looking into her clear brown eyes. There was understanding and acceptance there. "Please, hold me and be with me. Let's lay here and think about what a beautiful life we have."

His eyes were locked on to hers. She could see that he was fighting acceptance, she saw anger flare up and knew that it was anger at himself and probably God.

"Nathan, it's okay. My life before you was cold and isolated. I lived in a world and a home that never knew love or kindness. The only love I ever felt was from God, but He was far away and remote. I knew He was there and that He loved me, but I longed for a human touch and physical closeness. Your letters changed that. Coming here and becoming your wife saved me from that isolation and opened up for me not only our love and happiness, but a new and deeper understanding of God's love. Once I experienced your love for me and my love for you, I could understand God's love so much more clearly."

She smiled at him then, and watched as the anger and denial began to seep out of his eyes. What she saw instead was his love for her, with edges of sadness.

Nathan got up long enough to check the fire and shrug out of his shirt and shoes. He climbed in under the covers and they snuggled up together then. With his body warmth next to her, Andriette began to feel warmer. They spent the evening holding on tightly. Andriette slept some and they talked and remembered their lives together. They laughed when they shared how they'd felt that first afternoon on the train platform in Rawlins. He kissed her tenderly as they remembered their first night together. Each had moments of tears along with smiles and giggles. They told each other many times that they loved the other, and they shared deeply about what their love provided. Finally, calmness reigned, and both of them slipped into a quiet, restful sleep.

Chapter 28

August 22, 2007

At the same moment Hannah realized that she was not the only inhabitant of the cave, Travis' voice assaulted her from the growing dark outside. Night had fallen quickly, and there was only a tiny bit of dim, dusty light outside. Eyes wide open yet unseeing, Hannah raised the hand holding the rock over her head. She glanced first toward the back of the cave but it was so dark she couldn't see anything, then focused on the cave opening. What she saw there confirmed that Travis had indeed seen the cave. His flashlight beam bounced outside and inside the cave entrance, she shrunk back into the cave wall and remained in darkness.

"How clever of you," he was right outside, just inches from her, his voice quiet and clear, "you found us a place to spend the night together."

The hand holding the flashlight came into view. Hannah stood motionless, hoping that she might get a chance to use her rock. She tried to merge with the wall and become invisible. Silence prevailed for a moment longer. The flashlight beam explored cave opening, barely missing her. She kept her eyes on the hand holding the light. The circle of light then moved away from her and toward the interior of the cave.

When Travis realized what the light revealed at the back of the chasm, he made a guttural noise as the flashlight fell forward, its light bouncing crazily. Rocks crunched and skittered on the slope outside as he tried to get away.

Hannah was confused, not knowing what made him react this way.

Then a scream tore open the darkness.

Hannah dropped the rock she'd been holding and covered her mouth. The lion's strong shoulder brushed against her face as it exploded through the small opening and into the night.

Events became slow motion to Hannah. She heard the lion snarl and Travis' wordless yell. The flashlight lay about two feet from her on the cave floor. Its light seemed an intrusion after the profound darkness that encompassed the interior. Not bothering with the light, she climbed out through the mouth of the cave and then immediately scrambled up hill. She used her hands and feet to climb higher, to put some distance between herself, the cave, and the savage noises she continued to hear below her. When she reached a large tree at the top of the ridge, she stopped. The forest was silent. She crawled under the low hanging branches and nestled into the space they created at the base of the tree. Putting her back against the sturdy trunk, she listened. At first all she could hear was her own heart pounding, then it was quiet. The noises of struggle subsided. Night sounds returned. An owl hooted from a high perch. The wind gently rustled the tops of the trees. All else was silence.

Somewhere below her and not far away, the lion screamed again.

Hannah sat without moving. Unwilling to move from her shelter into the utter blackness of the night, she stretched her socks out over her pant legs so bugs couldn't crawl up her legs. Then, pulling her hand into the sleeve of her sweatshirt for protection from the points, she swept up pine needles from around her and piled a nice layer of them for insulation on her legs. She snuggled down into her sweatshirt and made herself as comfortable as possible. She tried to picture what happened after the lion left the cave. Did Travis stab her? Did she scare him away?

That long ago day when she and Dad studied the mountain lion's tracks over her own came back to her mind. Dad's words came back to her. "Today we connected with a marvelous beast, and that, Hannah, is a gift not many people get. That lion knows you, now she's connected to you. She will always recognize your scent, next summer and for years to come." Hannah couldn't help but wonder.

Chapter 29

August 23, 1907

Nathan woke just as the sky outside the cabin window was tinged with pink and orange. He lay still, not wanting to disturb the moment. The cabin was quiet. The forest outside the cabin was still lost in the silence of the night. No bird sang, no squirrels were yet up chirping and scolding through their day. Nathan closed his eyes and treasured the feel of Andriette's cheek on his shoulder. He realized the cabin bore a silence thick and unyielding.

He stirred enough that he could look down on his wife's face. She was beautiful and peaceful. Her hand was on his chest, the plain gold band encircled her relaxed and gentle fingers. He knew then that the silence he was hearing was her absence. Her body, which was as precious to him as his own, was here as it should be, but Andriette was gone.

He lingered for a bit longer, knowing that when he got up, his world would be different. He hesitated to take the first step on his new journey, so he lay there, memorizing every detail he could about how this moment felt. He allowed himself a time to turn off his thoughts about reality and to savor the final moments of having his wife in his arms.

When he got up, he hardened himself so that he could function. He had to find a way to sever the connection between his heart and his mind, so that he could face the tasks at hand. So, when he did get out of bed, he was all business. The room was chilly from the night. He washed his face in the cold water in the basin, and smoothed his hair. He dressed in the clothes he'd worn yesterday and pulled on his boots. He turned toward the bed, and tenderly pulled the covers up. He knew that he should cover her face, but he couldn't, so he tucked the quilt in under her chin as if she were sleeping. He felt dangerously close to letting his heart take control, so he quickly grabbed his hat and left the cabin.

It took him most of the morning at the sawmill to build what he needed to build. When he finished, he carried the box up to the meadow and went back for his pick and shovel. He stopped for water a few times, but did not go back into the cabin.

He didn't have to think about where to dig. It was intuitive. He sat for a moment with his back against the rock before he began. It was warm from the sun and it warmed his heart a bit. When the feelings threatened to get too much, he got up and began digging. The ground was loose due to the recent rains, but the work was hard in more ways than one.

He dug the hole wider than the box so that when he'd finished digging he could slide one end of it into the hole and then climb down himself and finish placing it. He made sure the box was level and then climbed out.

Nathan went down to the creek to wash up. He was dirty from his day's work, and bathed as best as he could in the cold water of the Haggarty. It was late afternoon when he returned to the cabin. He refused to allow himself to look towards the bed. He changed his shirt and pants. He wanted to be clean and neat. Only when his hair was combed and he'd checked his appearance in the mirror did he turn his attentions to the other side of the cabin.

He chose his favorite dress, the white one with the green sash she'd worn that first evening in Encampment with his family. He remembered how beautiful she looked that night. Shaking his head to clear the memory, he dressed his wife. He didn't know how to braid or put up her hair, so he brushed it and left it down. Sometimes he had trouble seeing what he was doing as the tears flowed freely, but he did manage to keep his focus on the job at hand and keep his heart at bay.

He carried Andriette and the quilt she and Lillian made up the ridge to her meadow and laid her gently beside the hole. He climbed down in and reached for the quilt, folding it and arranging it so the rough wood of the box was covered. Nathan took his wife in his arms for the last time and placed her gently on the quilt. He crossed her hands so that her wedding ring was visible then kissed her gently on the forehead. He reached for the lid to the box.

He finished his work with the shovel and stood for a few minutes staring at the bare ground and the rock. At last, he turned his back and looked out at the meadow. It was a view he'd seen often and loved nearly as much as she did.

Nathan Jameson said no words at the grave of his wife. His heart was numb. He had so many things to say to Andriette - a lifetime of things to say to her that he knew now would never be voiced.

As Nathan stood with his back to Andriette's grave, the sun's rays died. The sun itself and its light dipped over the western mountains and slowly seeped away. Twilight's blues and grays took over for the days' yellows and greens, and the world became dark for Nathan. He successfully kept himself focused on the work he needed to do this day, but now the work was done and he could no longer keep his heart in suspension. He watched the day become night and his heart passed from numb to angry. He was furious. This was not fair and it was not right.

How long he stood there he never knew, but the emotions of the past day assailed him and took over. He felt paralyzed by fear and anger. He wanted his wife back. He wanted to hear her laughter and see her face. What finally spurred him into movement was the shrill eerie scream from a mountain lion very nearby. Maybe she didn't like Nathan in her meadow at night, maybe she sensed that an ally of hers was gone from this world, or maybe she was oblivious to the things of man and was hunting. No matter her reason, the lion screamed with a ferocity that matched what was in Nathan's heart.

The scream of the lion moved Nathan. He picked up his pick and shovel and headed back to the cabin. He stood in the doorway and surveyed their home. It was so simple and rough yet it was everything he had ever wanted.

He went a little crazy then, knocking over the table and sending the cups that rested there crashing across the floor. He threw the china against the wall and pulled over the hutch. When he finished smashing and breaking everything he could, he was exhausted and sobbing. He sat on the floor amidst the wreckage of his life and railed at God and rocks and cold spring water until his anger was spent and he was calm. He didn't sleep, but prayed and pleaded and came to peace with God's choices through the night.

When the day arrived, he quietly but resolutely hitched his team of Morgans to the buckboard, tied Andriette's mare to the back, and prepared to drive away from the cabin.

Lillian heard the rig approach and stood out of the porch as the horses clomped into the yard. When she first saw the wagon from afar, Lillian hoped that Andriette and Nathan were arriving with joyous news of a child on the way. When she realized that Nathan sat alone and she looked at the grim expression on his face, her body iced over in fear. She struggled to accept the news he brought.

The man that climbed down from the wagon in front of Lillian's home was not the son she knew. He remained bitter and outwardly grieved only for a short while, but he never regained his easy laugh or his joy. After a season, Nathan was happy in a new way and found satisfaction in running the store and managing the sale of lumber to the store in Baggs. Lillian welcomed him into her home and they fell into a comfortable, quiet life. He became even more private and reserved. People in town respected him as an honest business man who dealt fairly with everyone. His friends knew him as a quiet man worth listening to.

Chapter 30

August 22, 2007

Carrie Warren entered the Encampment Grocery Store's front door at about four. The drive to Baggs over the mountain to see her mom had been pleasant, but something was worrying her. "Bob," she called.

"I'm in the back," her husband answered.

Carrie put her purse and keys under the counter and then noticed that Mrs. Stiles was choosing a head of lettuce from the cold case. Carrie greeted her then and the two women chatted. Bob appeared just as Carrie finished bagging Mrs. Stiles' purchases. He kissed his wife's cheek in a quick hello as Mrs. Stiles left.

"Did you have a nice visit?"

"Yes, Mother seemed much better today. She even knew who I was at first."

Bob took in the worried look on her face, knowing that watching her mother sink into dementia was hard on Carrie.

"Bob, when Harvey was here yesterday, didn't he say something about a man they were looking for?"

"Yeah, some guy from Rawlins."

"Why was Harvey interested in him?"

"Since Harvey is the Forest Service captain for the Sierras, he gets info from local police and sheriff offices. Apparently local law is looking for a guy who hassled some campers yesterday at Lost Creek Campground." Bob thought about the conversation, Harvey told him the man made some advances toward a woman camper but left when her husband and their dog returned to camp.

"Seems like Harvey said the man could be a convict that went missing from an honor farm near Rawlins."

Carrie turned to face her husband. "Did Harvey say the man was on foot, or does he have a vehicle?"

"I think he said he was last seen in an old pickup. Why all the questions?"

"Bob, when I drove over just now, there was a green pickup truck parked near the gate at the Harding cabin."

"I'll call Harvey."

Chapter 31

August 23, 2007

The tangerine dawn began to be replaced with blue when Hannah became aware of the sound of a man's rough voice. "Hannah!" Panic swept through her. Travis! She stayed concealed under her canopy of limbs until a second voice called, "Hannah Harding, I'm Harvey Layton from the Forest Service. We're here to help."

She stayed quiet and still until she could see a man in a dusty brown shirt and pants through the trees. She recognized the uniform as forest service and sighed with relief. She crawled out from her tree-tent and called out to the man. He turned and saw her then. He began making his way up to her as he spoke to someone on his radio.

Hannah brushed herself off. She wondered where her captor was and how the rangers knew to come looking for her. She was relieved that the ordeal was over for her.

Harvey Layton introduced himself again to Hannah and checked to make sure she was okay. Two other men soon joined them. She assured them she was only dirty, hungry and tired and gave them a quick, abridged version of the events of the evening and night she'd just spent. She was so drained and weary, she didn't notice their glances when she described Travis. She couldn't miss the incredulous looks on their faces though, when she told of sharing the cave with the lion and what happened there. Whether they believed all of her story or not, the rangers went into immediate action. Harvey Layton walked with Hannah back toward the cabin while the other two left in the direction she'd pointed.

As they walked, Hannah told her story again, this time in detail. Harvey interrupted her several times for clarification, and Hannah gave him all the details she could remember starting from the first time she saw Travis in Encampment to the final sounds she endured in the darkened forest. Layton quizzed her again about the cave and the lion. When she finished, she timidly added the story about her lion encounter when she was a teen. She shared with Layton her dad's thoughts about her connection to the lion.

As they neared Hannah's cabin, Layton filled her in on the man they suspected was her captor. His name was Travis Davisson. He was two thirds of the way through a nine year sentence for robbery and rape. Since he'd been a model prisoner, the authorities transferred him to a low security honor farm near Rawlins about six month ago. Last week, he walked away from the farm, stole a truck and vanished. Layton described the minor havoc Davisson created at the campground nearby and told her of the call from Carrie and Bob Warren that alerted him that she might need help.

When they reached the cabin, Harvey carried water for her and Hannah stoked up the stove. The ranger enjoyed a cup of coffee as Hannah excused herself to the bedroom with a basin of warm water and a towel and washcloth, which she sat on the bedside chair. She returned the porta potty to the closet and closed and locked the window. Fear returned to her in a wave. She swallowed hard and stopped tears. With resolve she shed her grimy clothes, washed up and put on clean jeans and a long sleeved shirt. She stood in front of the small mirror and brushed her hair, taking stock of the scratches on her face and the drawn look.

She returned to the kitchen and poured herself a cup of coffee as the radio crackled the news. The searchers found Travis' body in a draw about fifty yards from the mouth of a small cave. He had been mauled by a mountain lion. The rangers confirmed that the cave had been the lion's den. Tracks and signs definitely showed that Hannah's story was true. There was no sign of the lion. They were going to wait for the coroner. After some discussion the men on both ends of the radio agreed that using the Gulch road was the best choice. Harvey returned the radio to the holster on his belt.

"They won't go after her, will they?" Hannah was worried that they would decide to hunt the lion.

Layton looked at Hannah for a long time before answering. "No, I see no reason for us to worry that animal any more. She was only following her instinct."

"Her instinct?"

"Yeah," he smiled at her then. "Seems like she was just protecting her young."

Hannah wondered if he was mocking her and searched his face. He was serious.

Harvey's radio crackled again and he answered. The police needed to ask her some questions and get a statement. Harvey put the radio on the table and returned his gaze to Hannah. "They can meet us at my office in Encampment. I am certain that Milly can find a room for you to stay at her bed and breakfast if you'd like to stay in town." Clearly, Harvey didn't expect Hannah to want to stay at the cabin after all she'd endured.

Hannah looked around. This was Friday. She hadn't planned to leave the cabin until Saturday afternoon at the earliest to return to Denver. Once everyone left, would she be too scared to stay here alone?

She hesitated. She felt relatively calm, though she knew she should be scared. *Maybe I'm in shock and will fall apart later.* Hannah searched her feelings. She was shaken up, tired and sore from her night out in the forest. Even so, she felt okay.

"I think I'd rather have the officers come here, if they wouldn't mind," answered Hannah finally. "I'm not quite ready to leave."

Harvey looked skeptical but keyed the mike and gave the police directions to the cabin.

"They will be here in about an hour. Are you sure you are all right?"

Hannah met his eyes. "No, Sir, I'm not sure. I'm rattled no doubt, but the idea of leaving worries me." Harvey looked confused. Hannah went on, "I love this cabin, and I want to make sure I am not scared to come back here." He smiled and sipped his coffee, impressed with her pluck and determination.

Needing to be busy, Hannah began cleaning up. She shuddered as she picked up the plates and silverware on the table from her meal with Travis the night before. *I came so close!* She stopped herself in mid-thought, refusing to give in to the gnawing fear of what could have been. When the dishes were clean and in the drainer, she reached into the cupboard and found an apple but then realized she was very hungry. She rummaged through the cupboards and cooler and even though it was not quite noon, she soon had mac and cheese and hotdogs cooking on the stove. She and Harvey talked a little, mostly about the design and history of the cabin.

"I met your dad a few times," he told her. "He had a great reputation with the locals."

"He was a really good guy." Hannah agreed.

Harvey joined her in her comfort food meal. They were just finishing when they heard the sound of a motor.

"I'll need to go unlock the gate," Hannah said and started out. Harvey followed her. One officer had his head inside the old green truck on the other side of the fence. A second officer was looking at the license plate and talking on his radio. Hannah unlocked the gate and greeted the men.

Harvey shook hands with both and introduced them to Hannah as Robert Malloy and Dirk Packer.

"I've called a tow truck to come get the pickup," said Malloy, the taller of the two officers.

The shorter man, older with a tiny streak of grey at his temples, took control of the conversation. "This won't take too long, Miss Harding, but I need to ask you some questions and get a statement from you."

"I understand," replied Hannah. "Can we go back to the cabin? I'm a little cold."

They settled around the table in the kitchen, each with a fresh cup of coffee. Packer took notes when Hannah told the men what happened. At some point in the middle of her retelling, they heard the tow truck arrive. Finally, he asked her to sign the report and assured her that this would close the case.

The sun was close to the western horizon when the officers left. Hannah stood inside the fence with the lock for the gate in her hand. Harvey Layton hesitated before he got in his truck. "I'm a little concerned about leaving you alone up here. Will you be alright?"

Talking to the officers about her desperate dash through the trees made her heart race and her hands shake. Harvey saw that and could tell she was on a thin edge. Hannah sighed and regrouped. "I think I'm okay," she answered quietly. Trying to add a little lightness to the conversation she smiled and looked at him then. "I have a guardian lion outside, so what could happen?"

Harvey smiled and shook his head. "I'll ask the local sheriff's department and the highway patrol to stay in the area and keep watch around here tonight."

Chapter 32

August 23, 1909

As the second summer after Andriette died progressed, Nathan became more and more restless. He couldn't concentrate and he got angry easily. He'd done well working through his grief and learning to sleep alone again in his bed at his mother's, but as the hot sun reflected off the streets of Encampment, the colder and more stiff his heart felt.

Everything was different. Due to falling copper prices and bad investments by the North American Copper Company, the mine at Rudefeha closed in the summer of 1908. The smelter and the tramway fell silent and unused. The towns in the mountains began to decline and shut down altogether.

Nathan thought about his meeting with George Baker at the store last week.

"Well, George, it's good to see you. What brings you down out of the mountains?" Nathan asked him.

"I'm down for good, Nathan. Dillon is no more, I'm the last of the city's population to leave."

"What are you planning to do?" Nathan looked at the wizened old man.

"I'm staying here. I think this town needs a new watering hole, so I'm going to open a bar and see how that goes."

Nathan pondered that conversation as he straightened the shelves. He'd thought maybe after the hurt from

Andriette passed, he'd move back up to the mountains and go back to logging and running the mill. Now that Dillon and Copperton, Battle and Rambler were dead also, there was no point. He had a good life here, but he was having trouble letting go of what he used to have.

Nathan heard Lillian's footsteps coming from the back room. They greeted one another and she stopped beside her son and began organizing a bin of bolts.

They worked in silence for several minutes. "Do you think you could do without me for a few days?"

Lillian stopped and turned to him, "Where will you be?" She sensed his disquiet and searched for ways to come to his aid.

"I need to go back up to the cabin. I left some things unfinished up there."

"Will you be gone long?"

Nathan heard the unspoken questions behind the one she spoke. He turned to her with a sad smile. "Not long, I just need a break and to finish saying goodbye to my life up there. So much has changed since I lost her, Mom, and while I have settled in here, sometimes the mountains call me."

He left the next morning riding Daisy, with a saddlebag of food and a bedroll.

He passed the remains of Ellwood and entered the forest. His heart warmed as he rode, filling his lungs with pine and his ears with forest sounds. *The people may be gone from here,* he thought, *but the animals and all of nature have reclaimed what was rightfully theirs.*

Nathan didn't stop in Battle. The town was still active, though much smaller than when he'd last seen it. He skirted the town, but then turned off to take the high road. The trail took him up to Bridger Peak. Nathan picketed Daisy so she could rest and hiked the last few hundred yards to the pinnacle of the peak. He sat down to take in the panoramic view. Memories washed over Nathan as he looked out over the valley of his home. His eyes lingered on Battle Lake as he remembered the picnic he and Andriette enjoyed there during the second year of their marriage. He located the point of rocks that marked Haggarty Gulch and recalled the first time he'd travelled there with Andriette. He let his eyes feast on the beauty before him.

Down into the valley of ghosts, he thought as he approached Daisy later.

The high road led him over the top of the Continental Divide. He dropped over the ridge and into the trees. An hour later, it saddened him to see Rudefeha with its cable and transfer house standing empty. The bunk house, the offices and all the outbuildings scattered around the entrance to the mine were stoic and alone. The mine entrance itself was boarded up. Someone had painted "No trespassing" in red letters. The tram cables and stanchions sat waiting, the wind whining plaintively through the wires. Nathan and Daisy plodded through Rudefeha and continued a mile down the road into the valley. Dillon welcomed him with silence. The windows of the Dillon Hotel were vacant and dark. When Nathan had last been to Dillon the town was bustling with people, horses, mule teams and rigs. Today there was no life, no movement except a hawk wheeling silently overhead.

When he crossed the Haggarty and headed onto his own property, Nathan dismounted and led Daisy the rest of the way. He studied each tree and absorbed every sound. He circled the sawmill and decided that he'd send someone to retrieve the saw itself. The mule teams were all gone, so transporting the boiler would be expensive. Better to leave it here as a monument that he'd been here at all. His steps slowed and he struggled to breathe as the cabin came into view. Two winters had already given the forest a good start on reclaiming the cabin from him. The roof sagged at one corner. The door was ajar, as he'd left it the night he'd ridden away.

Nathan walked around the cabin before entering. He saw his home in two views at the same time, the way it had been and the way it now stood. He stopped at the garden, once full of promise and life. Finally, he entered the cabin. He regretted the chaos that he caused before he left. The smashed china and pottery, the overturned table and chairs all stood in silent accusation of his own destructiveness. He stood, lost in thought and memories, overrun with grief and longing. He gazed around the room, taking it in. He pictured Andriette standing at the stove, sitting on the bed, walking through the room and lighting up his life. He remembered the warmth of her laughter and the depth of her love for him. His eyes eventually fell on the carved box. It was laying upside-down on the floor at the edge of the bed. As he reached for it he spied a corner of Andriette's journal. It was also lying on the floor, mostly hidden by a tousled sheet. He lovingly picked them both up.

Nathan sat down on the bed and lost himself in the past, reading first from the journal, then sliding each precious letter from its envelope. He wiped his eyes so that he could absorb her words. The light in the cabin was dimming when he returned the letters to the wooden chest and gently placed the journal inside then re-latched it. Carrying the box cradled in the crook of his arm, he left the cabin.

Nathan untangled himself from the past as he began thinking of practical matters. He planned to spend the night, but couldn't bear the idea of sleeping in the cabin. He led the horse around back to the barn. After stowing the carved box in his saddlebag, he carefully unsaddled Daisy and brushed her down, thankful that the brushes and curry combs were still in the leather basket on the wall. He cleared a corner of the barn and laid out his bedroll. "You're going to have to sleep outside tonight, Daisy," he told the horse as he picketed her near the cabin. He made sure thick grass grew nearby for her to eat and walked to the creek to get water for her and himself. Soon he was sitting next to a warm campfire, eating stew and listening to the sounds as night fell in the mountains.

Revisiting grief had exhausted his body and brain. Nathan nodded by the fire for a while, then settled in for the night. He dreamt of Andriette and once thought he heard the old lion's savage call echo through the hills, but in the morning he couldn't distinguish between dream and reality.

Chapter 33

August 23, 2007

Hannah stood at the gate until the last sounds of Harvey's truck were swallowed by the winding road. She made her way back to the cabin, wondering still if she shouldn't pack up and leave right now. *If you go tonight, you might never return* she told herself. Inside the kitchen, Hannah picked up the coffee pot and started to refill her cup, then decided she really didn't need the caffeine. She rummaged through the cupboard and retrieved a box of mint tea, opened a new bottle of water, poured it into the tea pot and set it on the stove. She added three large pieces of wood to the fire. While she waited for the teapot to whistle, she walked around the cabin, closing the curtains and locking the windows and doors.

Soon, Hannah sat comfortably with a steaming cup of tea. Though the cabin was warm, she wrapped herself in a blanket, knowing that it wasn't the heat she needed but the feeling of security. Earlier Hannah told the rangers and the police what happened, but now that she was safe and alone, she allowed herself to relive each moment so that she could feel and come to terms with it all. Violence and evil weren't part of her life. She urgently felt the need to face the events of yesterday and find a path through it so it wouldn't have ill effects on her.

Wrapped in her cocoon, Hannah alternately cried, then shook. Her heart pounded as she remembered running wildly through the trees as the sun set. She held her breath as she thought of sliding into the mouth of the cave. Closing her eyes, Hannah felt the lion rush by her into the night.

She let herself dwell on that moment in time. After a while, she began praying, letting her heart be soft and honest. She recognized that she'd been through a dangerous yet awesome experience. She puzzled at the why of it all. Why had this happened was less important to her than why she had escaped, and why God had chosen to use a mountain lion as her rescuer.

Hannah was tired but not sleepy. She felt restless, but wasn't up for a walk outside. She ambled through the cabin and into her father's room – her room.

She thought maybe she could unwind by reading the *Doublejack*, but her eyes fell on the letter from her Dad and the carved wooden box on the desk. She picked them both up and moved back into the living room. She curled up in the blanket and adjusted the lantern.

Then she opened the box. It was filled with a stack of envelopes. She looked at the postmarks at first. All were from the early 1900s. Next, she began noticing that some were postmarked in Council Bluffs, Iowa. Those were addressed with a flowery, flowing script. There was no name on the return address, just the initials A.G. Other letters were post marked from Encampment, Wyoming. The return name was Nathan Jameson. His handwriting was strong and austere. She was eager to organize them so that she could begin at the beginning and read the letters through chronologically. She began sorting them into two piles. When she reached the bottom of the box, she was surprised to discover a small, leather bound book.

Hannah refilled her tea cup and settled back down. She returned the letters to the box and shifted her focus to the book. She opened the first page and began to read. The first page was written in the same strong, male writing as on the letters. *To Andriette, my love and my wife. Happy first anniversary. June 18, 1903 Love Nathan.*

Hannah was mesmerized by the first paragraph.

Today Nathan and I have been married one year. How surprised my father and aunts would be to see me sitting here so snug and content in our little cabin surrounded by these fierce mountains and enveloped in so much love. Maybe I didn't even guess that being a mail order bride could turn out so well.

Hannah was hooked. She read eagerly. The pages were filled with news and reflections and prayers.

This morning Nathan left for Rudefeha to take some timbers to the mine. The sawmill is quiet and the forest calls out to me. It's mid-afternoon, and I've climbed up to my meadow to spend a delightful hour or so sitting at my rock. I've been entertained by watching a fox and her kits play among the shadows on the other side.

About three quarters of the way through the volume, Hannah was surprised to come to the last entry. It was dated August 22, 1907.

Father, Nathan is a hardworking man, who sometimes can be a little rough around the edges. Lord, smooth off those edges so that he can glorify You more, and keep him near to you every day. Don't let him prosper just for the sake of being prosperous, but for Your sake. Thank you for this beautiful spot. Thank you for creating it, and thank you for sharing it with me. Lord Jesus, I ask you to bless any person who ever comes into this meadow or sits at this rock. Be real to that person. Draw them near to You. Protect them, and help them to find safety and comfort here and in You.

Hannah stared at the words. She thought about her dad's letter and his promise to be praying for her always. Could it be?

She felt the tension drain from her shoulders and neck and began to feel sleepy. Hannah slid into bed and was instantly fast asleep.

Chapter 34

August 24, 1909

As the sun began to announce itself, Nathan rose and made coffee over the fire. There was a job he needed to do this morning, and he started at it not long after the sun's rays broke through the tops of the eastern trees.

He rummaged through the tack in the barn and was relieved when he found the leather sacks he needed. One sported a small hole where a mouse had gnawed it, but Nathan knew the sacks would work. He patted Daisy then attached the sacks to each side of the saddle. They walked leisurely through the forest toward Haggarty Creek. Nathan enjoyed being in the woods. His grief was spent, and what remained was deep seated, silent joy. He knew he had been given the best this world offered, and he was thankful for it.

The woods were serene and peaceful. The sun ducked behind high, wispy clouds, though the day remained warm. Birds called quietly to each other from the tree tops, the wind whispered. At the creek bank, Nathan began selecting rocks one by one. He lifted each one and considered it. He chose rounded river rocks about the size of a loaf of bread and placed them in the leather sacks on Daisy's back.

When the bags were full and he thought there were enough, he led Daisy away from the creek. They hiked past the cabin and soon found themselves in Andriette's meadow. Nathan stopped to take it in. The flowers were blazing with a rainbow of colors. Bees and flies buzzed above them. Occasionally a hummingbird darted into view and just as quickly disappeared.

He made his way to the large rock at the western edge. Two summers had re-seeded the ground in front with a chaotic quilt of color. His smile was sad as he sat down to rest with his back against the warm granite face. He lingered there, harboring the memories of sitting here with his wife. He thought of her, lying beneath him in the dirt and rocks. He harbored so many regrets. He'd wished a thousand times that he would have come home the night he'd made the deal with Hardiger instead of staying in Baggs. He regretted that he didn't have a child of hers to comfort and to comfort him. He regretted he didn't have Andriette beside him now. His regrets weren't filled with bitterness or anger, only tinged with sad loneliness.

Nathan knew that she didn't need a headstone, the granite boulder she loved so much was better than any he could have ordered in town. But he did feel that she needed something to mark this as her ground. He rose and pulled the shovel that was tied to the saddle. He trenched two lines, each starting at the center of the boulder but away from it about three feet. The lines moved outward and away from one another. Then he dug a shorter trench to connect the two. Nathan spaced the creek rocks evenly down the length of each trench and then on the cross piece. He fitted them into the trench so that only about half of each rock remained at ground level. When he was satisfied, he backfilled the trench and tamped down the dirt around each rock to secure them. He was sweating when he stepped back and surveyed his work. The A was clear.

Nathan sat down once again with his back to the rock. Now that her resting place was marked, he rested.

Daisy shook her head and stomped. Nathan arose, returned the shovel to its place on the saddle, and led Daisy out of the meadow. He stopped at the spring and washed up, then made his way back toward the cabin. He didn't go inside again. He put the shovel back where he found it, then retrieved his bedroll and the saddlebag from the barn. He checked to be sure the carved wooden box was safely inside. Mounting Daisy, he headed back down the road toward Encampment. He stopped once and looked back at the abandoned cabin.

Chapter 35

August 24, 2007

Hannah slept more soundly than she'd expected. She awoke refreshed and calm, though as she got out of bed she realized she was sore. Her hand hurt where she scraped it when she fell in the loose rocks by the lion's den. One ankle was stiff; a dark bruise stained the other knee and her shoulder. She surveyed herself in the mirror. The scratch on her cheek was an angry red but not very deep. There was a handprint shaped bruise on her right arm where Travis grabbed her.

"You look pretty good, considering," she said to the woman in the mirror.

Hannah thought about the journal she'd been reading as she stoked up the fire and put water on to boil. There were two eggs left in the cooler and some sausage. She cooked them together in the cast iron skillet. She filled her plate, added the apple she hadn't eaten yesterday and went to the porch swing to eat. Her thoughts returned to the journal as she cleaned up the dishes and set everything right in the cabin.

Nearly an hour later, pushing a stray lock of hair off her forehead, Hannah looked around the cabin. The shutters were all secured in place. The porch furniture was stored back in the kitchen. She'd refilled the kindling box and brought in firewood, just like she and Dad always had. She carried her suitcase and the empty cooler to the car. On her last trip she put her overnight bag in the back seat and her purse and the carved box on the seat beside her in front. She locked the car, checked the doors and windows one last time. *Great! I have time for one last walk,* she thought.

She went back into the cabin and retrieved her rucksack. She smiled at herself as she thought about her dad telling her always to be prepared. There was no way she could be prepared for everything – she knew that now. There was no way she had control over anything but small details, either. Instead of railing against that thought, Hannah felt peaceful.

Hannah headed into the timber. She knew exactly where she wanted to go. She thought about the journal. Walking past the boiler, she listened to the wind and imagined what it would have sounded like up here to have a sawmill jarring the forest noises. The cabin sat, lonely and frail, in the dappled forest light. Once again, Hannah listened, hearing the echoes of a stove door clanking shut, or maybe someone sweeping the floor.

Soon she was sitting in the meadow, her back resting against the granite rock. The place was familiar, but things were different now. Hannah knew she was different. She considered first what she had learned of the woman who'd lived here. From now on she knew she'd call it Andriette's Meadow. The sun was warm, the sky was bright, deep blue.

Dear Father God, Hannah began, *I thank you. I have been really rotten to you and I am sorry. I don't know why You chose to protect me and keep me safe this week. God, was it my dad's prayers, or Andriette's or something else entirely? I don't know, but I know You are in charge. Thanks.*

Hannah sat and absorbed the peace and joy of the day around her. She let the flowers and sounds of the meadow envelope her.

***

Two hours later, Hannah was on Highway 230 heading out of Encampment. She finally had a cell signal and faced a long drive. It was time to call her mom. Hannah knew that first she needed to apologize and tell her mom how much she loved her, and then to share the week with her.

Author's Note

During my childhood I spent many summer days tramping around the town sites of Rudefeha and Dillon, Wyoming with my dad. We camped in an old green canvas tent and rode Haggarty Gulch road and many others on a vintage Harley Hummer motorcycle that Dad had fashioned an air breather cover for out of an old Skippy Peanut butter can. We greeted the sheepherders in the area, watched for deer and elk, and listened at night to the mountain lion scream. When I first arrived in Dillon, some of the cabins and building walls were taller than I. When we weren't actually there, I was reading and writing about it, spending time at the Wyoming State Archives, getting and reading old copies of the *Dillon Doublejack* as well as anything about the Grand Encampment area I could find. I have returned to the area, camping along the Haggarty many, many times since.

In these pages you will meet real people, who I have tried to be as accurate in portraying as possible. Malachi Dillon and Jack Fulkerson were brave and colorful men who contributed to the history of Dillon. George Baker was truly the last inhabitant of Dillon to leave. The Battle Hotel really was owned by Mrs. Kinsella, though Pearl is my own. Thomas Edison did travel to Battle Lake in 1878 and later returned to do some fishing, though the story of his getting the idea of the filament for the incandescent light bulb while there is thought by some to be more legend than fact.

The news and stories I quote and reference from the *Dillon Doublejack* are straight from its pages. Grant Jones was a creative and talented writer and his stories, both the factual ones and the imaginative ones, were well received and loved throughout the area.

Encampment still sits nestled at the foot of the Sierra Madres, the Grand Encampment Museum there is definitely worth the time.

Battle is no longer a town site per se, but it has been reborn as private owners have come in and built cabins there. Rambler, Copperton, Ellwood, Dillon and Rudefeha were towns that sprang up with copper mines, but remain now only as a few barely discernable foundations as the mountains have reclaimed them from man. All, I believe, are now on privately owned property. I have tried to depict the towns of Dillon, Battle and Encampment in the early 1900s as accurately as possible. The information about the aerial tram system is factual; it was an amazing feat of engineering for its time.

The grocery store where Hannah stops in Encampment isn't currently open, but the building that houses is it there. The main floor has been used for a variety of purposes including a bank and a store – which used to carry ice cream sandwiches. Lillian Jameson's house in the story is patterned after a great old house on the edge of Encampment with which I have always been enamored.

The Jameson family and Andriette and Hannah and her family are my creations.

Please check out my website for pictures and links regarding Dillon and the Grand Encampment copper boom as well as my weekly blog and other news and information at

www.donnacoulson.com

Acknowledgements

A thanks and a tip of the hat to these sources of information:

Bob Kelly at Chez Booze in Encampment for sharing pictures of the area

The Wyoming State Archives for copies of *The Dillon DoubleJack*

Candy Moulton's book *The Grand ENCAMPMENT: Settling the High Country*, High Plains Press, Glendo, Wyoming 1997

Wyoming Wildlife Volume LXX, Number 8, August, 2006 for the information about mountain lions

"Grand Encampment Mining District" from *Wyoming Tales and Trails* by G. B. Dobson,
http://www.wyomingtalesandtrails.com/rudafeha2.html

Grand Encampment Museum, Encampment Wyoming

Information regarding the Henry Draper Expedition and Thomas Edison came from various sources including Wikipedia.

Information about Thomas Edison and the invention of the incandescent light bulb: The Real Heroes Club website
http://www.theheroesclub.org/thomas_edison.php

Other titles by donna coulson:

Peaks and Valleys – Wyoming State Historical Society's fiction book of the year for 2017.

In 1894, Claire Atley's options are slim. She leaves her father's farm with limited resources and limited options. When a copper frenzy begins in Wyoming, she finds herself first in a desolate town called The Grand Encampment and then at the top of the world in a brand new boomtown called Dillon. On the journey she discovers her own precious mettle and finds love and faith to help her not only survive but triumph through life's peaks and valleys. In this companion novel to the award-winning *Mountain Time*, donna coulson takes us and Claire through the fascinating history of southern Wyoming's largest copper boom and gives us a look at one woman's struggle for faith and forgiveness.

The Archer's Perspective

Available September 2017

One Action
Three Reactions.
A beautiful fall day in Wyoming's Sierra Madre Mountains turns tragic and life-changing with the twang of a bowstring. Three people are involved that day and their responses to the challenges that follow reveal not only who they are down deep but how they see God.

Donna's novels are available in print or digital form at Amazon.

Follow donna on FaceBook @authordonnacoulson

Visit donnacoulson.com for pictures and information plus donna's weekly blog

Made in the USA
Coppell, TX
14 September 2020

37732365R20118